"Jeffrey, there a... know about my p...

"Things that I can't, for security reasons, tell you. The only thing you need to know," she continued, "is that you are in grave danger and I'm trying to help you."

The dead silence that followed her admission wasn't what she'd hoped for. Then Jeffrey burst into laughter.

"Okay," he said, "I'm sorry, but that's unbelievable. What are you up to?"

"There are some papers in my bag. Two pages. Take a look at those, please."

He heaved a long-suffering sigh. "Fine. Whatever." Paper crinkled as he considered the grainy picture someone had taken of him leaving the lab facility. "This is..." The second page listed his name, address, occupation and a full physical description. "What the hell is this, Olivia?"

"Someone has ordered a hit on you, Jeffrey." She didn't mention, of course, that they had hired her as the assassin.

Dear Reader,

I'm so glad you decided to pick up my book. I had a wonderful time writing this story and I'm hoping you will thoroughly enjoy it. This is my fourth Bombshell novel and I love writing about sassy, sexy women who have their cake and eat it, too!

Several scenes in this story are set in the Los Angeles area. Last summer I was fortunate to have the opportunity to travel to California for the first time. My daughter and I stayed in the Beverly Hilton and we did all the tourist stuff: toured the homes of the stars, took pictures of all the famous landmarks, went to Malibu (for chasing after more stars!) and, of course, shopped on Rodeo Drive. What a fabulous time we had!

We took our trip in July and I adored the perfect weather. I was amazed by all the beautiful blooming flowers and shrubs as well as by how friendly all the people were. That is one of the reasons I wanted to set the home and office of Dr. Olivia Mills in the L.A. area.

So, if you get the chance, go to California and see for yourself. I'm definitely going back the first chance I get. Who knows, maybe I'll see you there!

Cheers!

Debra

DEBRA WEBB
past sins

Silhouette®

BOMBSHELL™

Published by Silhouette Books

America's Publisher of Contemporary Romance

 **SILHOUETTE BOOKS**

ISBN 0-373-51410-7

PAST SINS

www.SilhouetteBombshell.com

Printed in U.S.A.

Books by Debra Webb

Silhouette Bombshell

Justice #22
††*Silent Weapon* #33
††*Silent Reckoning* #72
Past Sins #96

Harlequin Books

*Striking Distance
*Dying To Play

Code Red
Tremors

Forrester Square
Nobody's Baby

Double Impact
"No Way Back"

Mysteries of Lost Angel Inn
"Shadows of the Past"

Whispers in the Night
"Protective Instinct"

‡*Colby Conspiracy*

Vows of Silence

*A Colby Agency Case
†The Specialists
‡Colby Agency: Internal Affairs
**The Enforcers
††Merri Walters stories

Harlequin Intrigue

*Safe by His Side #583
*The Bodyguard's Baby #597
*Protective Custody #610
Special Assignment: Baby #634
*Solitary Soldier #646
*Personal Protector #659
*Physical Evidence #671
*Contract Bride #683
†*Undercover Wife* #693
†*Her Hidden Truth* #697
†*Guardian of the Night* #701
*Her Secret Alibi #718
*Keeping Baby Safe #732
*Cries in the Night #747
*Agent Cowboy #768
‡*Situation: Out of Control* #801
‡*Full Exposure* #807
***John Doe on Her Doorstep* #837
***Executive Bodyguard* #843
***Man of Her Dreams* #849
Urban Sensation #864
Undercover Santa #879
Person of Interest #891
*Investigating 101 #909
*Raw Talent #916

DEBRA WEBB

was born in Scottsboro, Alabama, to parents who taught her that anything is possible if you want it bad enough. She began writing at age nine. Eventually she met and married the man of her dreams. When her husband joined the military, they moved to Berlin, Germany, and Debra became a secretary in the commanding general's office. By 1985 they were back in the States. With the support of her husband and two beautiful daughters, Debra took up writing again, looking to mystery and movies for inspiration. In 1998, her dream of writing for Harlequin came true. You can write to Debra with your comments at P.O. Box 64, Huntland, Tennessee 37345 or visit her Web site at www.debrawebb.com to find out exciting news about her next book.

I've met a lot of terrific ladies in my life who would definitely fall into the Bombshell category, but not one with a truer heart than Vicki Hinze. Vicki possesses every single trait that epitomizes a Bombshell heroine. I feel privileged to call her my friend.

Chapter 1

Never count on anything to last.

From the large window in reception Dr. Olivia Mills watched uneasily as her final patient climbed into his Bentley and drove away from her West Hollywood office.

Other than talking to the dead, this particular patient was a class act. Well dressed, well mannered, wealthy. Unfortunately, like far too many Hollywood residents, his love life might never be stable. But then, that meant job security for her. As long as people needed a sounding board her calendar would stay full.

That, she mused, was the upside of high anxiety.

Though her private practice wasn't that large, she had half a dozen or so eccentric has-been stars on her patient list as well as a few she considered to be regular civilians—in other words, not employed in the entertainment industry. Most, in or out of the business, she had inherited from the man who'd retired after four decades in this very location.

Olivia had been fortunate enough to meet him during the leasing process and they'd formed an instant friendship—an extremely rare development for her. The whole father-figure notion hadn't been lost on her at the time.

Her new friend had recommended her to all his patients, ensuring a grand start to her new endeavor. That he'd passed away only a short time later had reiterated a couple of theories that she'd operated under for a significant portion of her life—never depend on anyone, never count on anything to last.

If she were like most in her current field of expertise she would have her own shrink with whom to discuss that very issue as well as a multitude of others. But the past sins that had formed her deeply rooted cynicism were far too great to lay at anyone else's door.

Tearing away from those dark thoughts, she locked the front entrance and tidied the magazines on the table near the sofa. She surveyed the small reception room, noted the drapes were looking a little drab and out of date. She'd have to do something about that before long. It was hard to believe she'd been here three years already.

A tiny knot formed in the pit of her stomach when

she thought about how comfortable she'd gotten with this life.

Never count on anything to last.

"Enough, Olivia," she muttered. Looking forward was the only direction she allowed nowadays. No exceptions.

Before turning out the lights she checked the soil in the pots of salmon-colored geraniums to see if they needed water. Good to go for another day, she decided as she clicked off the light. Exhaustion nipped at her heels. She'd had a full schedule, one interesting client after the other. She had to smile as she considered some of the stories she'd heard. She did love her work. Loved her life, as well.

And that was the truly scary part.

"Stop it," she muttered. *Stop thinking stupid thoughts. Stop overanalyzing and contemplating the worst.* Her period had come and gone this month. There was absolutely no reason for her to be obsessing like this. Depression wasn't her style, no matter how hormonal she felt on any given day. The right kind of training could teach a person to block most any discomfort. And she'd had all the right training.

More ancient, irrelevant history she didn't want or need to think about.

Five minutes was all she needed to straighten her office and dictate the results of her final session. The patient continued to experience panic attacks related to the death of his last liaison. He'd been in one of those mega-intense relationships where physical intimacy overwhelmed his entire existence to the detriment of his mental well-being.

Olivia had experienced that kind of relationship personally and could understand how one could get caught up in the incredible sensory rush. It was like a drug. The memories evoked by the thought were immediately stuffed back into their designated compartment before regret and too many other emotions to name could take root and ruin what should be a perfectly good evening.

What was wrong with her today? She hadn't had this much trouble maintaining a proper attitude in more than two years. Listening to that last patient go on and on about the powerful bond with his lover had obviously prodded loose far too many pieces of her own past. There was simply no other explanation.

After a deliberate mental adjustment and checking of her calendar for the next day, she locked her desk and files, made her way out the side exit and climbed into her Audi. She lowered the convertible top, backed out of the alley that served as a parking lot and pointed the car toward home.

Home.

Even after three years that felt a little foreign.

In her former life she'd moved around a lot, seldom spending more than a few months in any one place. She'd had a home base, so to speak, but nothing she would have called *home*. Certainly not in the way she considered her small ranch-style house in the Hollywood Hills. It was her first real home. The admission brought with it another prick of uncertainty. Why all the creepy feelings of imminent doom? Apparently she needed a long, hard run to clear her mind. Extreme physical exertion would likely do the trick. Maybe she'd spent too much time behind her desk lately.

She slid her Oakleys into place and sped along Santa Monica Boulevard. The sun felt amazing and she abruptly wished she were on the beach soaking up some rays. She definitely needed a vacation. Maybe that was the real problem. It was the middle of July already and neither she nor Jeffrey had made time for an escape.

She'd have to speak with Jeffrey about getting away. It was past time. Their combined work schedules were grueling. Between his research at the lab and her high-maintenance clients, they barely had time to manage dinner on a regular basis.

Olivia glanced at her watch. Just past 1800 hours.

Her teeth clenched as she cursed and amended her assessment—6:00 p.m. was what she'd meant.

The tiny gold heart and delicate matching chain lying against her throat abruptly felt like a rock pressing down on her. She would *not* think about the past.

She took the turn up Mount Olympus, scarcely letting off the accelerator. The oleander and casa blanca lilies and tropical hibiscus were in full bloom. The colorful displays in pots and flower beds were eye-catching and filled the breeze with their sweet smells. She wished she knew all their names. She'd never been much of a gardener. Now that she had the time and place for it, she felt aeons behind on what she should know—what everyone but her appeared to know. Her neighbors gave the impression of having been born with green thumbs.

Maybe she'd get the hang of domesticity eventually. Meanwhile she'd enjoy the other benefits of being a "regular" civilian.

Summer in California, in particular, was nice. Very nice. She'd grown to love it here. Her love for the place had prompted a sort of nesting instinct—at least, the closest thing she'd ever experienced to one.

Braking hard, she took the turn into her narrow drive. A smile spread across her face at the sight of hummingbirds floating away from her bougainvillea. Thankfully the previous owner had cultivated a thriving landscape that required little know-how. All she had to do was remember to do the watering and occasionally pluck a few weeds.

Jeffrey's practical Saturn was already parked in the drive. She hoped he'd started dinner. That was one of the perks to having a live-in relationship. You didn't have to do all the cooking or cleaning.

She and Jeffrey had been living together for six whole months, dating for nine. A record for her. The realization still startled her. It was her first long-term commitment of that sort. He wasn't the love of her life, but she enjoyed his company and the sex was quite adequate.

Memory attempted once more to intrude at that

juncture but she kicked it back. She definitely wasn't going there. Now or ever.

Once the convertible top was locked into place, she slid out of the seat and headed inside. The pleasant smell of her favorite white-wine sauce filled her nostrils the moment she stepped through the front door. Linguini and chicken, a staple of Jeffrey's culinary repertoire, would be on the menu. In addition to the pleasant aroma, classical music greeted her, the elegant notes playing softly in the background and making her feel immediately more relaxed.

"I'm home!" She almost laughed at the cheesy way she sounded. If she'd only tacked on the "honey" she would have been a living, breathing cliché. Olivia Mills had never been accused of being a stock quotient. Had that changed in the past three years along with everything else about her life? Evidently so. But there were definitely worse things. A lot worse.

"In here!" accompanied a rise in the tempo of the brass, strings and ivory keys.

Her stomach rumbling, she followed the smell into the kitchen. Hesitating at the door, she watched Jeffrey, engrossed in the preparation of a rich green salad. He paused in his work to dump the linguini into boiling water then turned back to slice fresh tomatoes into thin slivers just the way she liked them. He had very nice hands. Long, artist fingers. But the thing she liked best about him was his infinite patience and unconditional trust.

Two things she'd never been able to master herself. Her patience had never been that noteworthy, unless she was billing by the hour. And trust, well, she'd never trusted anyone. Still didn't…but she tried. Jeffrey made her want to try.

"Rough day?" he asked without looking up.

"Not so bad."

He would ask her about lunch next.

"Did you have lunch with Liz?"

"She had to cancel." Liz was a colleague with whom she lunched once or twice each month. They were about the same age, both single. The other woman was pleasant but, to be brutally honest, they had nothing in common other than profession. Still, socializing within the profession was expected. Fitting in dictated certain behaviors on her part.

With her and Jeffrey it was basically the same conversation every night. How was your day? Anything interesting happen at lunch? The only variable was whether she got home first to start dinner. Comfortable. Easy.

A trickle of trepidation seeped into her veins, making her pulse rate increase and reminding her that complacency was a weakness. Weakness was dangerous. All afternoon she'd been experiencing these sensations that alternated between urgency and hesitancy. Strange.

"Too bad. I understand she had some gossip to pass along," Jeffrey said, tugging her full attention back to him. He glanced at her and smiled that familiar, charming smile that had drawn her to him in the first place. "Wine?"

She nodded and he stopped his salad preparations long enough to pour her a stemmed glass of chardonnay.

Annoyed that she couldn't stay focused tonight, she moved to the island and accepted the drink. "Gossip?" she asked, feigning interest. Her heart rate's refusal to drop back to a normal level frustrated her further.

Jeffrey placed the glass in her hand. "She's leaving her position at Whitworth Clinic."

Olivia made the expected sound of disbelief. "What brought that on?" She listened as Jeffrey launched into the explanation that Liz's significant other had no doubt passed along to him. In Olivia's experience, men did a lot more talking about secrets than women did. She found this apparently common phenomenon among the civilian population amusing—or maybe it was just that her life before had been so vastly different. Whatever the case, there were times when she actually managed to feel intrigued by the juicy gossip floating about their social circle.

For some reason, today just wasn't one of those days. Today she had to pretend. It had been so long since she'd had to do that....

"What about you?" she asked when he'd completed his dissertation on the subject of their mutual friend's abrupt decision to move to a rival clinic. "Anything interesting happen in the world of research today?"

Dr. Jeffrey Scott was employed by one of the country's foremost pharmaceutical research corporations. Though the corporation was strictly private—no government affiliations whatsoever—what he did deep within the bowels of that facility was top secret. That was the part of their relationship that she related to the most readily.

He shrugged. "Nothing notable."

She hummed a note of acknowledgment and sipped her wine. "I think I'll change."

He reached for the next vegetable in need of slicing. "Ten minutes. Don't be late."

She produced a smile and turned away from the domestic scene.

This was her life. Comfortable. Easy. But there were times, like now, when she felt out of place. As if she didn't really belong here in this house... with this man. She downed a gulp of wine in hopes of bolstering the facade of happiness she'd worked so hard to veneer into place over the past three years.

"Don't think about it," she scolded softly as she tossed her purse onto the table in the hall. Allowing a patient's session to prompt this much anxiety was not her usual response. She was stronger than this.

The journey through her home was taken slowly. She surveyed every detail as if for the first time. Anything to get her mind off these ridiculous feelings of apprehension.

She had updated the house immediately after moving in. Gutted the place, actually. Sparing no expense, she had wanted a relaxing yet sophisticated living space. The interior decorator she'd hired had taken great pains with the decor and the furnishings had accomplished that goal. Using *things* and everyday decisions to fill the emptiness in her life had worked as an excellent distraction at first. Eventually it was not enough. She'd turned her attention elsewhere.

Dating had proven a practical trial for occupying her time for a while. However, no one had lasted beyond date number three until Jeffrey. She tossed her double-breasted suit jacket onto the king-size bed in their room and strode into the walk-in closet to find something more comfortable.

It wasn't that she'd fallen in love with Jeffrey. He'd simply fit nicely into the life she'd created for herself. He was reliable, kind and always considerate. He made no complicated demands. Simple was her new motto, after all.

Pink silk lounge pants and a matching camisole replaced her skirt and button-up blouse. The tile of the en suite bath felt cool beneath her bare feet, a welcome respite after wearing stilettos all day.

Once she had taken the pins from her French twist, she brushed through her long dark hair until it glistened around her shoulders. If she really took the time to consider her reflection, she would have to admit that she looked the same as before. Her hair was longer and darker, but otherwise she'd changed very little. Same green eyes. No additional wrinkles to speak of for a woman closer to forty than thirty. It was everything else in her life that had altered.

She hissed a breath of impatience. Why couldn't she stop this? She hadn't had this much trouble focusing since…since the beginning.

She grabbed her empty glass and headed back to join Jeffrey.

He'd set the dining table. Flowers, candles and the lovely white bone china they used every day. He placed the salad bowl in the middle of the table next to the linguini and white-wine sauce before he looked up.

"You need another drink."

He moved to her side to remedy that situation without her having to say a word. That was another thing she enjoyed about Jeffrey. Making her happy appeared to be his single goal when they were together. She should be grateful.

She was.

"Smells heavenly." She thanked Jeffrey for the refill and settled into the chair he pulled out.

He took his own seat directly across from her and lifted his glass. "To us." He smiled as their glasses clinked. "And a lovely evening."

She returned the smile and drank deeply from her wine.

Now was all that mattered.

Her new life…this moment.

The unmistakable sound of her cell phone chimed from the hall. She groaned.

"Don't answer it," Jeffrey suggested, looking mildly annoyed at the intrusion.

Olivia sat her glass down. "I shouldn't." She took a deep breath and rose from her chair. "But one of my patients is having a crisis. If he needs me…"

Jeffrey rolled his eyes but said nothing as she left the table without finishing the statement. He understood her dedication to her work even if he didn't like it at times. He was every bit as dedicated as she was.

She walked to the hall table and fished her phone from her bag. Jeffrey was right. She shouldn't answer. If it was one of her patients, he could leave a message.

The display flashed an icon she didn't remember seeing before. She frowned as she attempted to remember what it meant.

Then she knew.

Never count on anything to last.

Chapter 2

For ten seconds Olivia couldn't breathe.

This was impossible.

She told herself to inhale. Instinctively she reached up and fingered the necklace that served as a constant reminder of all she wanted to forget.

"Is everything all right, Olivia?"

Her gaze shot to the dining room where Jeffrey stared at her, concern marring the smooth features of his intelligent face.

She swallowed. "I have to take this."

Before he could give her a disappointed look for allowing the intrusion during dinner—during *their* time—she escaped out the front door.

This was not a call forwarded from her office

number or her home number or any other number represented by some part of her present life.

This was the past calling. An old cell number she'd once used as a lifeline…a number she'd tried for three years to forget but could never bring herself to let go.

By the fifth ring she had reached the edge of her driveway. She flipped open the phone, her heart pounding. "Yes." It was a miracle her voice didn't quaver.

"Sheara?"

The earth shook beneath her, or maybe it was her rigid frame doing the shaking. She tried to steady herself but the name reverberated through her like the aftershocks of a major quake.

This wasn't possible.

She licked her lips. "Yes."

"I have a problem that requires your kind of special attention. You were highly recommended." He cleared his throat. "I would like to arrange a meeting as soon as possible."

Olivia blinked, glanced around the neighborhood to ensure she hadn't attracted any unnecessary attention. It wasn't dark yet but the temperature had dropped significantly, making her shiver.

Or maybe it was the call sending that bone-cold chill rushing through her veins.

Sheara didn't exist any more. How the hell had this guy gotten her old number? This wasn't supposed to happen. She'd kept that number for one reason only…

"Sheara? Are you there?" The caller cleared his throat again. "Maybe I have the wrong number."

"No." She said the word more sharply than she'd intended. "You have the right number." What the hell did she do now? She was a psychologist, for Christ's sake. She didn't do *this* anymore.

Sheara was dead.

She'd been dead for three years.

She bit back the need to ask how he'd gotten her number. "Where would you like to meet?"

There was only one way to find out who this guy was and how he'd gotten her number. Meet him. Right now. Tonight. This couldn't wait. Her heart rate climbed with each new realization.

"The location is your choice…right? That's what I was told."

Olivia squeezed her eyes shut and forced herself to take another breath. He was right. She had to focus. "What's your location? And I'll need a name." She tried to block the sound of her heart thundering, pumping blood so fast it roared in her ears. What was she doing? This could be a trap. But why? She'd been out of the business for three damn years. The woman she used to be was dead.

His hesitation told her he wasn't too keen on the idea of giving his name or his location. "Ned…Soderbaum. Chicago."

It was seven-thirty now. Approximately a three-hour flight. Assuming he could get one in the next hour, midnight would be the earliest meeting time.

"If you can get a flight—"

"My company has…I own a jet."

Well, okay then. Flight scheduling wouldn't be a problem. Where to meet? It wouldn't be a good idea to have him come to Hollywood. Wait. What was she worried about? This was Los Angeles County, including Los Angeles, Beverly Hills and dozens of other mass-population centers. There was an endless supply of anonymous places to meet and far too many people to make her easy to single out.

"The pier at Santa Monica. Midnight."

More hesitation. "How will I know you?"

"What will you be wearing?" she countered.

"Business suit…ah…navy."

And you'll stand out like an American tourist on a nude beach in the south of France, she wanted to say. "Won't work, Mr. Soderbaum. You want to look like a local. Wear khaki shorts, a white T-shirt and a red baseball cap. I'll find you." At that time of night the pier would be pretty much deserted.

"I guess I can do that."

"Don't forget the sneakers and the retainer fee."

"I'm…I'm not sure on that last part. I didn't get a clear idea of your fee."

She blinked, suddenly uncertain what to say to that. She remembered well the going rate three years ago, but that would have changed by now.

"Ten now, fifteen later. Nothing larger than a twenty."

Olivia didn't wait for his acknowledgment. She closed her phone, ending the call.

She stared at the compact device for an endless moment. What had just happened here? Confusion cluttered her thinking process. Too many questions filled her head. No answers.

Doing a three-sixty right there on the sidewalk she surveyed her quiet neighborhood. The smell of freshly mown grass lingered in the air. Somewhere down the street a dog barked. Two houses to the right of hers the owner paused in his shrub pruning long enough to wave. Children balanced on their skateboards on the sidewalk on the opposite side of the street.

Nothing had changed.

She stared at her brick home with its clean, crisp coat of white paint…her silver Audi…Jeffrey's blue Saturn…the lush, colorful landscape all around her. This was her life. She and Jeffrey were supposed to be having dinner. Then they would watch a little television and go to bed. Maybe they would have sex, maybe they wouldn't. And tomorrow everything started over again. Work. Home. Sleep. Uncomplicated. Safe.

Her gaze dropped to the phone in her hand.

Until thirty seconds ago.

"Can't you at least have your dinner before you go?"

Jeffrey watched from the bedroom door, none too happy that she had to leave so abruptly.

"You'll probably be there most of the night," he pressed. "Even practicing psychologists need to eat, Olivia."

She pulled the lightweight black sweater over her head and tugged it down her torso to cover the waist-band of the black slacks she'd chosen. "I'll be fine, Jeffrey. Don't worry. I'll pick up something at the hospital cafeteria."

He continued to loiter in the doorway, looking un-settled and uncertain as to whether he should attempt to come up with a more compelling argument. "You'll call when things calm down?" The way his posture relaxed told her he'd resigned himself to the inevitable.

It didn't happen often, but occasionally one of her patients would do something radical like take a few too many pills just to make someone believe he or she had intended suicide. The attention received was the point. Episodes such as those were the rare occa-sions when Olivia had to attend to a patient in the hospital.

She ushered a smile across her lips for Jeffrey's sake as she stepped into a comfortable pair of black flats that, fortunately, had rubber soles. "Of course I'll call." He always worried about her.

"I'll clean up the kitchen."

Olivia waited until he'd had sufficient time to get back to the kitchen before she returned to the walk-in closet. She closed the door and moved to the back of the closet. Dropping to her knees she dragged out several shoe boxes until she encountered the one stashed at the very back of her side of the closet, behind all the others. The one she hadn't touched in three years.

Her respiration slowed as she removed the lid of the box. Her fingers wrapped around the sturdy butt of the Beretta 9mm. She tested its weight. Her pulse reacted. Without hesitation she snapped in a clip and tucked the Beretta into the waistband of her slacks at the small of her back. She grabbed the sound suppressor and an additional fifteen-round clip before putting the box back into place behind the others.

With the accessories slipped into the right pocket of her favorite black silk jacket, she pulled it on. Though southern California nights could get pretty damn cool, the jacket was more to camouflage her weapon than for comfort. She stared at her reflection in the full-length mirror and took a deep, steadying breath.

She hadn't fired a weapon in thirty-seven months. Hadn't participated in a covert maneuver in even longer.

She had to be out of her mind to go through with this.

But what choice did she have?

Whoever had given out her number—whoever knew she was still alive—had to be ferreted out and contained. She couldn't pretend this away. Sheara had far too many enemies to take that route.

Olivia was at the front door before she considered that she couldn't simply leave without saying goodbye. Jeffrey had to believe this was a routine call-in for a patient who'd been admitted to Cedars-Sinai's psych ward for observation after a possible suicidal episode. The one or two other times she'd had to do this would serve as proper reasoning for her inability to offer a time she could be expected back home.

If she came home…

Jeffrey blew out the candles as she approached the dining room. He'd already cleared their plates and the basically untouched salad and entrée he'd gone to so much trouble to prepare.

"I'll call you later to let you know how it's going." She told herself the statement was about consideration for his feelings. Work he could understand, even if it intruded at an inopportune time. But if she were totally honest with herself she'd admit that she'd gone this extra step to ensure he didn't grow suspicious. The habit was deeply ingrained.

Just like old times. How many lies had she told to the people in her former life's orbit? She'd have lied to her own mother had she not been long deceased. Her past life had been built on a careful framework of deception. Lies were all that had kept her alive.

She suppressed the shudder that rocked her insides.

"I'll warm something up for you when you get back."

"Thanks, Jeffrey."

She had to go. Telling him not to wait up was pointless. He would…he always did.

As she walked out the front door and down the

paved path to her car, all six senses alert to her sur-
roundings, she couldn't help thinking that nothing
would ever be the same again.

Her new life was over.

The only question was…why?

The drive to Santa Monica took only forty-five
minutes. Traffic was light. She didn't hurry. She had
plenty of time. Arriving early would afford her the
opportunity to find a reconnaissance position.

The night security would be lurking about, but it
wasn't unusual for people, tourists in particular, to
come to the pier at night to enjoy the moonlight on
the water.

The park rides, the shops and the restaurants
would all be closed by midnight but there would be
plenty of lighting. She would need to take great care
in selecting her position. If terminating this guy became necessary, she didn't want any witnesses.

As darkness descended fully and the crowd thinned,
Olivia took a position between a closed fast-food
tourist trap and a bait and tackle shop. The smell of
overcooked hot dogs and frying oil lingered in the air.

During the day, the pier was crowded with locals
as well as tourists. As midnight approached, only a
lone soul or two lingered on the massive wooden
pier. A few others walked along the beach.

Olivia waited in the shadows, analyzing anything
that moved. She saw her target's arrival from a con-
siderable distance as he passed under a light en route

from the parking area to the wide planked board-walk. Khaki shorts, white T-shirt and red baseball cap, just as she'd requested.

She couldn't make out his face yet. He strolled along somewhat hesitantly as if this might have been his first visit to the pier or maybe he was just afraid of being in a strange place after dark. The pockets of his shorts didn't bulge, indicating he carried nothing about which she needed to be concerned. What appeared to be a video-camera bag hung on his right shoulder.

As he unknowingly neared her position, he paused and turned all the way around, evidently looking for anyone who might be watching him. With his T-shirt tucked neatly inside the waistband of his shorts, it was obvious that he wasn't carrying a weapon as she was.

When she'd made out the details of his face she confirmed that she hadn't met him before, but that didn't mean he wasn't trouble.

When he moved just in front of her position, she stepped out of the shadows. "Mr. Soderbaum."

He gasped and whipped around to face her. Even in the dim lighting she saw his face pale. "Sheara?" He was either a very good actor or scared witless.

Before she began her questioning, she patted him down to ensure he wasn't wearing a wire or any other sort of listening device. With the more unde-tectable microfiber jobs, it wasn't an easy task, so she took her time. She might not be in the business any-more, but she tried to keep up with the latest gadgets.

When she'd satisfied herself that he was clean, she asked, "Is the bag for me?"

He nodded jerkily. "Yes. Sorry." He swung the camera case off his shoulder and offered it to her.

Olivia accepted the case and opened it for a quick peek. Hundreds of crisp twenty-dollar bills were stacked inside, but that wasn't her concern at the moment. She checked for tracking and listening devices and found none. Whether that was good or bad, she wasn't precisely sure.

"Excellent."

"Do you need to count it?" He glanced around nervously. "What if someone sees us?"

"I'll count it later." She closed the case and slung it over her shoulder.

He nodded. "Of course. If it's not all there you won't go through with the job."

She ignored his comment. "Before we go any further, I have a few questions for you, Mr. Soderbaum."

Uncertainty claimed his expression once more. "I thought I wouldn't have to answer any questions. I just give you the money and information and the job gets done." He wasn't as old as she'd anticipated. Forty maybe. And right now he looked thoroughly terrified.

"Not those kinds of questions, Mr. Soderbaum," she assured him. "I never accept an assignment without verifying certain things, like who recommended me."

"I don't know his real name. I got the recommendation in a chat room."

Man, this guy was stupider than he looked. "You're lucky I'm not a federal agent, Mr. Soderbaum."

Taken aback and obviously startled, he asked, "Why would...oh." Realization appeared to dawn on him then. Soliciting murder was a serious crime, usually carried a life sentence. The muscles of his throat struggled as he attempted to swallow. "I hadn't thought of that."

"Fortunately for you, I'm not." That part was definitely true. She opted to get straight to the heart of the matter before pushing for his source. If she made this guy too nervous he might balk. There were certain elements she needed to know and the identity of the target was one of them. "Why don't we get down to business?"

He nodded, the movement as uncoordinated as a bobble-head doll's.

"I'll need the specifics on your target."

"Of course." He reached into his back pocket and pulled out what looked like a couple of folded sheets of paper. He hesitated before giving them to her.

"Is there a problem, Mr. Soderbaum?"

"You don't look like a killer," he commented quietly.

She leaned closer to him, making him catch his breath all over again. "Have you ever met a killer?"

He shook his head with enough vigor to do internal damage.

"Perhaps you've met several and simply didn't know it."

His eyes widened, then he blinked twice as he

appeared to comprehend that a response to her statement wasn't necessary. "How do you usually, ah—" He cleared his throat. "You know, take care of the situation?"

"Do you have a preferred method?"

"Not at all. I just want it done."

"I understand."

He hunched his shoulders and let them fall in a shrug of uncertainty. "How long will it take?"

"A few days. I'll need time to assess the target and to select the best time and method for elimination."

Ned Soderbaum gulped.

Keeping a close eye out for anyone else who might attempt to advance upon their position, she let him hang on to his papers a moment longer and pressed him for the crucial details she needed. "Mr. Soderbaum, before we can seal this deal, I will need the name of your source. I don't accept clients without verifying their source."

He tried to hold her gaze but couldn't handle the pressure, so he stared at a covered rack of postcards instead. "He's not that difficult to find. He's always in the chat rooms. I don't know his real name, but his screen name is Phantom."

A new wave of shock went through her. "You're certain about that?" The shock abruptly started to evolve, heading toward fury. This had to be a setup, wire or no wire. Her instincts moved to a higher state of alert in anticipation of coming complications. The necklace she wore felt hot against her skin.

Her client nodded. "I've talked to him several times. He said you were the best. A perfect record of kills."

Olivia struggled to conceal her building anger. Allowing him to take note of her out-of-control emotions would be a mistake. "Once I've confirmed that information I'll set things in motion."

"Excellent." Soderbaum glanced around nervously. "Here." He held out his papers. "This is the information you'll need."

She accepted the folded pages. "You understand that once this assignment has been set in motion there is no backing out. You can't change your mind."

He wet his lips. "Yes, I understand. I want this done as quickly as possible."

"All right." Olivia unfolded the paper and studied the full head shot of her target. What her eyes saw made her sway, but she braced herself before her client could pick up on her stunned surprise. Focusing intently to ensure her hands didn't shake, she shuffled to the next page where the target's name, address and other stats were listed.

The name and address matched the face but she couldn't analyze that right now. Her movements deliberate, she refolded the pages and slid them into her jacket pocket.

"I'll post a personal ad in the *Chicago Tribune* when the assignment is completed. The ad will contain a number for you to call for the final instructions on depositing the remainder of the fee. If you fail to make the deposit, you'll be my next target. There won't be any place you can hide from me."

Doubt clouded his expression again. "Don't worry, I'll make the deposit, but how will I know it's you?"

She eased into the shadows. "You'll know."

Olivia retreated behind the surveillance deck the police used. The route she chose was dark and she was pretty damn sure her client wouldn't attempt to follow her.

Thankfully he didn't.

When she reached the parking area, she remained out of sight until Soderbaum climbed into his vehicle and drove away.

She got into her Audi and drove back to Hollywood.

She needed some distance…some big-time perspective.

After three long years of evading the past, it had come back to haunt her.

Sheara, aka Goddess of Death, had been awakened by an old enemy. One she would not allow to betray her a second time. Her fingers tightened on the steering wheel. Whatever his reason for intruding on her new life, she would stop him. Hell, he shouldn't even know she was alive.

Forcing her attention on the road, she made the journey back to her house on Mount Olympus in record time, despite her evasive route. She had fully anticipated a tail. If there had been one, she'd lost him.

She parked behind Jeffrey's car and went inside, locking the door and resetting the alarm.

Jeffrey was asleep when she entered the bedroom. She didn't need a crystal ball or a hidden camera to know he had waited up until his body could no longer deny its need for sleep. Even as frustrated as he must have been when she didn't call to let him know how things were going, he'd likely waited up far longer than was reasonable because he cared. Something else she couldn't bear to think about just now.

She didn't bother with a light, just tucked her loaded weapon beneath her pillow and stripped off her clothes before climbing into bed naked. The subtle scent of Jeffrey's aftershave felt familiar and somehow comforting, as did the contrast of the cool sheets and his warm skin.

She lay there, the minutes ticking slowly by, wondering how this could possibly be happening. Sleep was out of the question at this point. She had to be ready for anything. Why would *he* do this? The idea that jealousy might play a role made her furious all over again. How the hell was she supposed to handle this? She had no contacts…nothing.

If she located the Phantom again he would be the one she would execute. Not an innocent target used to draw her back into the line of fire.

Gritting her teeth was the only way to hold back the litany of raging expletives hovering at the back of her throat. He had no right to do this. She'd already given up far too much because of him. The urge to jerk the necklace loose and throw it as far as she could was a palpable thing…but some idiotic, vulnerable female part of her wouldn't allow her to break that link.

He had given it to her.

A soft ring of the telephone shattered the silence. She reached for the bedside extension before the second ring could disturb Jeffrey.

"Hello." She kept her voice low, barely a whisper. Silence.

"Hello." Still nothing. She didn't immediately hang up. Just listened. Someone was there—she could sense the presence—but he didn't speak. He never did.

Then came the click signaling the end of the call.

Was the fact that the call had come only minutes after her return from meeting with Soderbaum significant? Possibly. She hung up the receiver. But this was not her first anonymous call. It was always the same. The phone would ring. She would answer and the caller would remain silent as if the single word she had uttered was the only reason he'd called—to hear her voice. There was no pattern to the calls. They came when they came. She had no idea who the caller was, but she wondered…foolishly.

Just as she often felt someone watching her.

And now she knew why.

He was back.

She couldn't begin to imagine his objective just yet, but he would have one. Her fingers toyed with the one token she had kept from her past as her gaze drifted to the man sleeping next to her. She could not allow her past sins to intrude on his present. He had no idea who or what she had been three years ago. She had to stop this plunge toward disaster before Jeffrey got hurt.

She closed her eyes and summoned the image of the target Ned Soderbaum had given her a ten-thousand-dollar retainer to eliminate.

Why on earth would anyone want Jeffrey dead?

Chapter 3

Unable to sleep, by 4:00 a.m. Olivia was on the Internet attempting to track down one Ned Soderbaum. It wasn't easy since she had to do this the hard way, without any useful contacts.

She tugged up the shoulder of her silk robe, annoyed that it kept slipping down. Or maybe just annoyed. Who would have thought that after three years she would need this kind of information? It wasn't as if a dead woman could attempt to log into the CIA's database without causing a stir.

Nope. She was on her own. Even if her old user name and password worked, she wouldn't risk revealing herself. Not if she wanted to stay alive. Apparently one too many people already knew she was alive. Why contact her now? After three years? She was too much of a realist to believe that the resurrection of her old persona was simply a coincidence, especially considering the target.

Olivia shifted the mouse and clicked, sending Google into yet another search. While she waited for the results she glanced at her weapon lying on the desk in front of the flat-panel monitor.

A cold sweat formed on her skin. Her heart rate jumped into a faster rhythm.

She hadn't taken a human life in over three years. Could she still do it if the necessity presented itself?

A shaky breath rushed past her lips, making her doubt her ability to accomplish the feat she had once performed with scarcely a thought. That had been a different life…she'd been a different person.

The search results spilled across the screen, drawing her attention back to her task. One or two Soderbaums. Lots of Neds. But no Ned Soderbaum of Chicago. Her gut told her the guy didn't exist. But she had to be sure. The proof was right in front of her. No businessman with enough clout to own his own jet would be thriving without at least one hit on Google.

She could hack into the Social Security Administration's system as one final stab. She'd already looked at the Illinois DMV database and found nothing. What was one more infraction? She would cover her tracks pretty well, going through an anonymous user ID on Hotmail. Still, a state-level intrusion like the DMV records wouldn't readily evoke an all-out search for the perpetrator, but a federal breach would bring on the big dogs. Homeland Security's Net Defense Unit would follow the inevitable tracks until they located this very computer.

It was a chance she'd have to take.

A few more clicks of the keys and she had her answer. No Ned Soderbaum in Illinois, period.

The man had either lied about his name or he didn't exist. If he'd simply lied about his name, that wasn't such a big deal, but if he was using an alias, that was a whole different matter. Not using his real name at the moment she asked would have been about fear. Using an alias carried the idea of premeditation, a strategic maneuver to mislead her. Which screamed of a setup.

Still, if this was an Agency-sanctioned operation, why hadn't they done their homework and given the guy a history to go with the alias? Ensuring a cover was verifiable was Spy 101 stuff.

There was only one answer. Because they wanted her to know she'd been made.

Or…the real threat could be to Jeffrey, and whoever had sanctioned the operation had no idea that research scientist Dr. Jeffrey Scott lived with a former CIA assassin. That didn't make sense, either, since Soderbaum, or whoever the hell he was, had used her former code name…had mentioned an old enemy. Not to mention that in order for that concept to fly, she was back to the idea of a coincidence and she was a total nonbeliever in the theory. Not when *she* was the hired assassin.

She knew of only one way to get to the bottom of this.

Olivia leaned back in her chair and let go a heavy breath. She'd have to contact Hamilton.

The name ricocheted through her. David Hamilton had been and still was the deputy director of the CIA's field operations. If an op was under way he would know about it. But why hadn't he warned her if she was in danger?

After all, the fact that she was even alive was his doing. Why fail her now?

Too many questions, not nearly enough answers.

It would be daylight soon. There were things she had to do. She grabbed her Beretta and strode into the bedroom. Jeffrey still slept soundly. After placing the weapon into her handbag, she sat down on his side of the bed.

"Jeffrey." She shook him gently, then turned on the bedside lamp. "Jeffrey, we need to talk."

She wasn't entirely sure how she would get him to go along with her plan, but she had to convince him somehow. Both their lives likely depended upon his cooperation. Though at this point she couldn't say for an absolute certainty whether this was about him or her. He was a research scientist at a top pharmaceutical corporation. It wasn't out of the realm of possibility that someone had targeted him for some reason related to his work, government affiliated or not. Still, the involvement of her former identity had her leaning more toward something far less straightforward.

The moment his eyes opened he took note of the time on the alarm clock on the bedside table not twelve inches from his head. "It's early." He shifted his groggy attention to Olivia. "Is something wrong? How's your patient?"

With a weary smile tacked into place, she lied, "He's stable and thoroughly apologetic for causing the fuss." Evidently Jeffrey thought she'd only just returned from the hospital. Remnants of the lie she'd just told soured in the back of her throat.

Jeffrey scrubbed a hand over his stubbled jaw. "Aren't they always? Did you just get in?"

She shook her head. "I've been sitting here for hours thinking." That part wasn't entirely untrue.

He eased up onto his elbows and eyed her a bit more closely. "Something is wrong."

A barely discernible lift of her shoulders gave him the hesitant impression she intended. She knew Jeffrey better on certain levels than she'd ever known any man. She discerned what made him tick, how he would respond in any given situation. The nine months they'd shared, coupled with her extensive training on how to analyze a target, ensured she could read him like the proverbial open book. Though she would definitely categorize him as passive, sensitive, definitely a beta male, he was intensely protective of her feelings.

The quintessential nerd in school, he'd suffered at the hands of bullies during childhood, making him ultrasensitive to the needs of others. Maybe that was one of the reasons she'd been so drawn to him. He was the exact opposite of who and what she had been. Kind, patient, overly considerate even. She was counting on those very qualities right now.

"I think I need to get away."

Concern stamped out the last remnants of sleepiness in his eyes. "Are you thinking of a change in our relationship?"

He didn't have to say "breaking up"— she read the dreaded deduction on his face. That would be his initial conclusion. This was Jeffrey's first live-in arrangement, as well. His lack of experience in the area of relationships was, however, related as much to his dedication to his work as to his being an introvert.

"No. It's nothing like that. I just need to get away. I guess last night's episode was the final straw. I'm tired. We haven't taken a vacation all year. Do you think you could get away for the weekend?"

Relief and no small amount of hope flooded his expression. "I don't see why not." He scooted up to a sitting position. "It's Friday. There isn't anything on my agenda that can't wait until Monday. I'm certain they can manage without me for a day." He smiled, traced the tip of one finger along her cheek. "A restful weekend would be good for both of us."

Olivia's relief matched his, though for completely different reasons. "Great. We'll leave right away."

His ready agreement set part one of her plan in motion. She told him to pack for a rustic weekend, the location to be a surprise. Jeans, casual shirts and hiking boots. He didn't question her suggestions. Probably assumed they would escape to Zuma Ridge for hiking or Sullivan Canyon for mountain biking. She hoped he would continue to be so cooperative. The next couple of steps would likely raise his suspicions. But she couldn't worry about that just now. One step at a time.

Olivia packed for survival, something she hadn't done in more than three years. She was beginning to hate that number. Suddenly everything in her new life was a reminder of the way things had ended three years ago.

Jeans, cotton Ts and a couple of long-sleeved cotton blouses, emergency items like bottled water and first-aid materials. She went into the closet and got the last clip she had on hand for the Beretta. After clearing the right corner of the back of her closet, she tugged the carpeting loose from its tack bar. The envelope was right where she'd put it three years ago after the new carpet had been laid. Inside the envelope were a passport, driver's license and two credit cards issued under an alias she had hoped she would never have to use.

She dumped two pairs of shoes from a designer shopping bag, folded the bag neatly and went back into her bedroom. She stashed the cash, the shopping bag and other items in her handbag. Before packing the retainer fee she'd gotten last night, she transferred as much as she could to the various pockets of the clothing she wore and some into her handbag. After a quick search beneath the bathroom sink for a couple of disposable rain ponchos and the pepper spray she'd almost forgotten about, she was good to go.

"I've loaded my bag in the Audi."

Looking up too quickly at the sound of his voice, Olivia cracked her head on the edge of the counter. She hoped like hell her instincts would sharpen as she attempted to keep stride with her former ways. Otherwise they might not even make it out of the city.

"Are you sure you don't want to take the Saturn?" His lips stretched into a lopsided grin. "It fits with rustic a bit better than the Audi."

She rubbed at her head and manufactured an answering smile. "Don't worry. I have a plan for that."

He eyed her speculatively. "There's no way I can talk you into sharing our destination?"

She shook her head. "I want to surprise you."

He moved his shoulders up and down. "Okay. This is your adventure."

Just keep that attitude, she mused silently.

When her sufficiently sized overnight bag was loaded alongside Jeffrey's, Olivia slid behind the wheel. She'd already canceled her appointments for the day and Jeffrey had called his assistant.

Olivia kept a close eye on the rearview mirror as she drove to the airport in Burbank. It didn't take that long, less than an hour. Her companion didn't question her destination until she entered long-term parking.

"Are we flying? You didn't mention that."

She cut him a sidelong look that she hoped came off as seductive and secretive. "You'll see."

The amusement glittering in his brown eyes signaled that she had once more alleviated his niggling suspicions. "This is getting more interesting all the time."

When they entered the airport, luggage in tow, rather than going to a ticket desk, she headed for the Hertz counter. The line wasn't that long but she dropped her bag on the floor about thirty feet from the counter.

"Do you mind watching the bags while I get the car?"

"Absolutely not." He held up his hands. "And I won't even ask why we need a different car."

Good. He was still happy with the game. As brilliant, albeit shy, as Jeffrey was, he was still a man, and the promise of sex combined with mystery overrode a great deal of common sense.

"Guard those bags," she ordered with enough suggestion to have him glancing down at her bag in wonder. She'd never met a man yet who didn't love sexy lingerie. He didn't need to know that the most important things the bag actually contained were the rest of the cash Soderbaum had given her and another clip for the Beretta. She definitely didn't want to lose those. She had no idea what she might have to buy or who she might have to bribe before this was over. The shooting part she'd just as soon not think about.

Taking a quick look around, she left Jeffrey with

the bags and herded up behind the half dozen other people in the rental car line. The agent on duty didn't waste time. He moved through the customers quickly enough to impress even Olivia.

When it was her turn, she asked, "What kind of SUV do you have available?"

"Do you have a reservation?"

Olivia shook her head. "I'm hoping that won't be a problem."

Studying his computer monitor, he clicked a few keys. "Hmm." He rubbed his chin. "I have an Explorer. Will that work?"

"Perfect."

She gave him the driver's license and credit card for Jill Smart. She signed the paperwork and he instructed her on which shuttle to take to pick up the SUV.

A few minutes later she had the keys to the blue Explorer. Jeffrey commented on the size of the vehicle as they loaded their luggage into the cargo area, then even offered to drive. She knew her luck with his ready cooperation was about to run out.

"I'll drive. I have to make one more stop before we're on our way."

"Breakfast? I'm thinking we'll both need our energy." He glanced at his watch. "Stopping for breakfast would give me a chance to check my e-mail for yesterday's lab results."

9:00 a.m. She could eat. Funny, she hadn't thought about food until he brought it up. Maybe falling back into her old persona wasn't going to be as difficult as she'd first thought. Her focus had gotten a little keener in the last hour or so.

To keep him happy she cruised through a drive-through and took care of both their needs. Even if she had no appetite, she knew she should eat. He was a bit disappointed since he'd had a sit-down breakfast in mind, but her decision hadn't kept him from pulling out his BlackBerry and checking his cyber in-box.

She took the long way to her next stop in hopes of avoiding more questions, but she should have known that wouldn't work.

East L.A. wasn't exactly Brentwood, and no matter what neighborhood she drove through to reach her final destination or Jeffrey's preoccupation with remote-accessing his files, there was no way to hide the fact that they'd entered a whole different world. One where Doctors Olivia Mills and Jeffrey Scott did not belong.

"Good heavens, Olivia, where are we going now? I thought we were bound for a weekend in the mountains. Please tell me," he said, his voice teasing, "that you're only drawing out the foreplay."

"This won't take long, Jeffrey, I promise."

He didn't look totally convinced but he didn't put up an argument.

Though it had been years since Olivia had carried a weapon the way most women would a stick of lip gloss, she wasn't oblivious to the world around her. At times she'd driven through neighborhoods just like this to get a better grasp on where a patient had come from. Just because most of her patients were somewhat affluent now didn't mean they always had been. A few had clawed their way up from the gutter.

To better understand their way of reasoning, she'd wanted to make herself fully aware of the environment in which they'd grown up. So she wasn't entirely lost on this side of the city. Certainly she watched the news and read the newspaper; there wasn't any real question as to where she would find what she needed. The only question was whether she would survive the encounter with those who did the selling.

She parked the SUV in front of a shop she recognized, not from its name but by what she saw in the front display window. Iron bars shielding reinforced glass. Warning signs that a guard dog was on the premises and that neither soliciting nor loitering would be tolerated.

"A pawnshop?"

A civilian would think that. The sign on the window even said so. But Olivia knew better.

"I'll be right back."

"Wait." Jeffrey put his hand on her arm. "I don't like this, Olivia." He looked around at the dilapidated and deserted storefronts and the few pedestrians loitering in doorways. "This looks dangerous, even in daylight."

Unfortunately danger had already found them. He just didn't know it yet. If he would only stay cool a few more minutes. They were almost out of here.

She needed to get him out of this city. She needed to contact Hamilton as quickly as possible. Time was their enemy.

More lies. "Don't worry, Jeffrey. The man who owns this shop is a relative of the patient I was with last night. I just need to make sure he knows to stop in the hospital and check on his cousin. Family is very important during a crisis. I'll only be a minute."

He reached for the door handle. "I'll go with you then. I certainly don't want you going into a place like this alone."

Damn. Not good. "Look, Jeffrey, this guy is skittish, as you might imagine." The determination in those brown eyes told her that wasn't going to be a good enough answer. "Bottom line—" she punted "—it comes down to doctor-patient privilege. I can't really talk about the case in front of you. I'm certain you understand."

That he understood. But he still didn't like it. He surveyed the street again. "I'd feel more comfortable if you didn't go in. Wouldn't a phone call suffice?"

"I promised my patient I'd go see his relative personally. It'll only take a moment." She leaned forward and glanced first one way then the other. "Besides, I'm not so sure it would be a good idea to leave the vehicle unattended in this neighborhood."

A sigh hissed past his lips. "I suppose you're right. But—" he looked directly at her "—for the record, I don't like this."

She squeezed his hand. "I promise I'll make up for putting you through this."

He shook his head in defeat though a smile toyed with the corner of his mouth. "All right, you win, but be careful. I'll be watching the door. If any hooligans go in after you, I'm coming in."

"Good idea." Olivia grabbed her handbag and climbed out. "I'll be back in five minutes tops." She noted the hooligans he referred to as she strode quickly to the shop entrance. Five, possibly six young men. If the city was open for business, so were they. Gang members probably, judging by their appearance. She'd parked almost directly in front of the entrance. She should be able to keep an eye on things out here and still do her business. She'd rather have taken Jeffrey inside with her, but she couldn't do this with him there. He would definitely freak. She needed him far, far out of his comfort zone before she allowed him reason to give her trouble about her decisions.

The owner looked up as the bell above the door jingled. Olivia took a moment to glance back at Jeffrey, then performed a final swift visual sweep of the street. The handful of characters keeping the sidewalk from being totally deserted looked exactly like trouble, but nothing she couldn't handle.

"This ain't the Salvation Army."

Olivia turned to the shop owner who'd spoken. A comedian. Great. She walked to the counter. "I need to preview your arms."

He laughed and held out his tattooed limbs for her

perusal. "Whatever gets you wet, honey. I have another limb that's inked, too, if you'd like to see it."

"Your firearms," she clarified. If he'd had any question about her seriousness, the lethal stare she turned on was ample answer.

"You got a reference?" He looked uneasy now. Uncertain whether to provide the requested service, not quite sure he wanted to risk turning her down. California gun laws were some of the strictest in the nation, including a ten-day waiting period to buy a firearm. His guardedness was understandable.

She plopped her handbag on the counter. "You see this Louis Vuitton? Three grand." She held up her right hand. "You don't even want to know what this Rolex set me back."

He didn't look impressed or convinced.

"I have money to spend, my friend, a lot of money. Now, are we going to do business or do I need to go to the next block?"

He sent an anxious look at the door. "You could be a cop."

"Please." She grabbed her bag and hefted it onto her shoulder. "I don't have time for this shit. Show me what you've got."

Another glance at the door. "I'll have to lock up and you'll have to go in the back with me."

"No way. Give me a description of your inventory. Better yet, I'll tell you what I want. You can bring it out to me in this bag." She reached into her handbag and retrieved the carefully folded shopping bag.

The owner made a choking sound that might have been a laugh. "You want me to fill your Neiman Marcus bag with guns?"

"Do you have a problem with that?"

All signs of amusement disappeared. "How do I know you have cash?"

She took the wad of cash she had in the right pocket of her jeans and smacked it onto the counter. "I need ammo for my 9mm Beretta. Binoculars, a hunting knife and maybe a .32 for backup. Oh, and I'll need some metal handcuffs if you have them."

He nodded, still a little uncomfortable with the transaction. "Need any night vision?"

Her spirits lifted. Definitely. "How much?"

"Three more on top of what's on the counter and I'll set you up with everything you've asked for."

Left-pocket contents as well as what was in her handbag joined the twenties on the counter. "That's as good as it gets." She'd just dropped nearly four grand on his battered counter. He'd have to be happy with that.

All signs of uneasiness were gone now, replaced by greed and hunger. He reached for the cash as well as her shopping bag. "Three minutes is all I'll need."

She held on to the bag a moment before letting it go. "Three minutes is all you'll have if you try to fuck with me." The tone was all Sheara...one she hadn't used in a very long time.

The owner nodded and rushed to the back of his shop, the Neiman Marcus bag in hand.

Olivia moved to the door and checked on Jeffrey. No one appeared to have approached the SUV.

Once they were out of this town she would breathe a lot easier.

In less time than he'd proposed, the shop owner returned from his pilgrimage to the back of the store. He'd hardly made a sound, but she'd heard him. Her old instincts weren't gone for good.

"Everything you asked for." Careful to support the bottom of the bag, he settled it onto the counter. "You should take your stuff and go. *Now.*"

She approached the counter. "As soon as I've inspected everything."

The muscles of his throat worked as he struggled to swallow. "Suit yourself."

The .32 was brand-new. Plenty of ammo. Binoculars, good ones. The handcuffs jingled as she picked them up. "Keys?"

He nodded. "In the bag. Seriously, lady, you gotta get outta here."

"In a minute." She dropped the cuffs into the sack and reached for the coup de grâce, the night vision. Military. Seriously illegal but the best on the market.

"Excellent." She hefted the bag into her arms.

Neither of them spoke as she exited the shop. No "come again" or "thanks for shopping with us" followed her out the door. But she hadn't expected either.

She hit the remote unlock button and deposited her purchases on the floorboard behind the driver's seat.

"I was beginning to get worried." Jeffrey looked relieved that she'd returned to the vehicle. One glance at the guys still hanging out on the sidewalk a little farther up the block had him urging her to hurry. "Olivia, I think you should get in now so we can get out of here."

She closed the back door and climbed into the driver's seat. "I'm in. I did a little shopping while I was in there."

Too engrossed in what might happen next, Jeffrey didn't comment on the idea that she'd shopped in such a place. He depressed the lock button and heaved a relieved breath. "I feel immensely better now."

It appeared he might have spoken too soon. As she started the engine two of the men from up the block pushed off the wall they'd been supporting and headed her way.

"Olivia, where's that pepper spray you carry?" Jeffrey braced one hand against the dash and reached toward her purse with the other.

She grabbed his hand before it reached its destination. "Let's just get out of here." After a quick glance in the rearview mirror, she shifted into Reverse and floored the accelerator.

The Explorer lunged backward. She didn't slow down until she'd reached the end of the block. She shifted into drive with a jerk and executed a U-turn in the middle of the street. Her foot slammed back onto the accelerator and they headed away from the jerks who had stopped chasing them and now stared after the Explorer.

It would have been difficult to say whether the guys simply wanted to have a good laugh by scaring them or if they'd intended more. No point hanging around to see. Her money was on the former. It was the perfect setup. Let the pawnshop owner sell the goods, then steal them back. He could sell the same items over and over. Who was going to report him? Certainly not those, like her, desperate enough to buy weapons illegally.

"That was…" Jeffrey twisted around in his seat, the safety belt restricting his movements, to verify that they weren't being followed. "Amazing. I've never seen anyone back up that far—at that speed—without crashing!" He craned his head to the right and then to the left as if she'd given him whiplash while accomplishing the feat he'd just witnessed with such admiration. "I'll never again doubt your ability to get out of a sticky situation."

"I only knew I had to get out of there."

Yet another lie. She'd had extensive training in just that sort of maneuver in her former life.

Jeffrey chuckled. "I guess we're just lucky you had the presence of mind to think of it, much less do it."

She made a noncommittal sound. Luck had nothing to do with their survival thus far, but she would take all the good fortune fate decided to toss her way.

"At least we can breathe easy now," he said as they took an exit to the freeway. "We're out of the woods."

He just didn't know. They were far from out of the woods. The real trouble hadn't even started yet.

Chapter 4

"It's 2:00 a.m. We've been driving for seventeen hours, Olivia. Why don't we stop for the night? You must be completely exhausted. I know I am and I haven't driven the first mile."

Olivia had pushed this mystery-getaway excuse just about as far as she could. Jeffrey's anticipation had given way to impatience. They'd been traveling east on I-40 since leaving L.A. She had nineteen, maybe twenty more hours to go before reaching her destination.

"We'll stop in Memphis."

"Tennessee?"

Looking at him in the dimly lit interior of the car wasn't necessary. His incredulous tone said it all.

"Yes, Memphis, Tennessee."

He sat up straighter in his seat.

Not a good sign. But then she'd known this moment would come. That he'd been working on his BlackBerry for hours was likely all that had gotten her this far without more questions. Jeffrey often got lost in his work.

"I'm sorry, but something is very wrong here. Why are we driving to Memphis, Tennessee? We should have flown if going cross-country was your plan." He shifted so that he looked directly at her profile. "Are you sure there isn't something you need to tell me?"

At least he still sounded open to whatever she had in mind, if not understanding of her reasoning for choosing this particular mode of transportation. She would love to have flown, but she needed to be armed. The two didn't mix. There was a time when she'd had contacts all over the country but she couldn't count on any of that now. Trust was hard earned in the business of assassination and black market transactions. Absence did not make the heart grow fonder in this instance. Being out of the network for a time then reappearing abruptly got one killed more often than not. And there was the fact that public transportation carried a higher risk of being tracked. It was impossible to walk into an airport or train station without a camera recording one's every move. Even bus stations had beefed up security. All of which was a good thing, unless one's intent was getting away unnoticed.

The dealer she'd done business with in L.A. didn't know her, past or present. She would not risk running into trouble with an old contact. *Never depend on anyone, never count on anything to last.* The last time she'd depended on anyone she'd lost everything…including her life.

"You're right, Jeffrey," she confessed, aware she'd gone as far as she could with her current ruse. "Something is wrong." All she had to do now was figure out a convincing story.

"Did you lose that patient last night? Is that what this strange behavior is about?"

She could see where he might think that. Careful to keep the necessary attention on the road, she hedged, "I didn't lose a patient, but there was an incident. I don't want to talk about it right now. I just want to drive. Can we do this at the hotel in Memphis? I'll explain everything then."

He didn't answer immediately. She knew he was weighing her words, wrestling with a decision that would please her while still placating his logic. Jeffrey was a very careful man. He never did anything random. His nature was exacting, logical and ordered. Taking a last-minute weekend away was about as spontaneous as he got. But those were just more of the traits she'd appreciated about him. She'd needed reliable.

"I'm worried about your emotional stability just now, Olivia. This isn't like you at all."

Well, damn.

"But we've come this far. I don't see any reason

why we can't continue to Memphis," she offered, appealing to that firm logic. "We can go to Graceland," she teased, hoping it would lighten the moment.

"This is no joking matter. I feel strongly about getting to the bottom of what's motivating this irrational behavior. You must tell me what happened."

He was right about one thing. This wasn't like Olivia Mills. This wasn't even like Sheara. Olivia wasn't at all sure she could be that person again. But somehow she had to try…for Jeffrey's sake as well as her own.

She hadn't wanted to do this part yet, but he wasn't leaving her much choice.

"Jeffrey, there are things you don't know about my past that I can't, for security reasons, tell you. The one thing you need to know is that you are in grave danger and I'm trying to help you."

The dead silence that followed her admission wasn't what she'd hoped for but there it was.

Then he burst into laughter.

Well, hell. She kicked back the fatigue clawing at her and kept her mouth shut while he got it all out.

"Okay." He fought to control the outburst and to catch his breath. "I'm sorry, but that's unbelievable. What are you up to?"

She weighed whether or not to attempt convincing him further. When they didn't return to L.A. by Monday he wouldn't think any part of this was funny. Did she go ahead and give him the whole truth now and deal with the reaction, or did she wait until something happened to persuade him? Men were visual creatures after all.

"We should go back to L.A.," he said, still chuckling under his breath. "This really isn't fun anymore, Olivia. We could stop, talk this out, get some sleep and head back later this morning. Not that getting away isn't a good idea, but clearly there are issues here that need to be resolved."

Looked like the truth wouldn't wait.

"There are some papers in my bag. Two pages. Folded. Would you take a look at those, please?"

He heaved another of those long-suffering sighs. "If it makes you happy." He clicked on the overhead interior light on his side of the compartment and dug around in her bag.

"Olivia."

She cringed. Damn. She'd forgotten about the Beretta.

"There's a gun in your purse." His head came up; his gaze bored right through her. It wasn't necessary to look at him. She could feel it. "Why is there a gun in your purse?"

"It's for protection, Jeffrey. Lots of people have guns." That sounded lame even to her.

"Why do you suddenly need protection? We live in the Hollywood Hills! If our zip code didn't make you worry before, what's changed? Was there a drive-by shooting I don't know about? Was one of the neighbors burglarized? What's going on, Olivia? We've never owned a gun before. I don't understand this."

"No drive-bys as far as I know," she answered calmly, though she doubted her calmness would prevent his hysteria from escalating. "No burglaries or anything else out of the ordinary. This isn't about where we live. Ignore the gun. What you need to see are the papers."

Another of those long awkward moments of silence. Finally paper crinkled. She caught a glimpse from the corner of her eye as he unfolded the two pages Ned Soderbaum had given her at the pier what felt like an eternity ago.

Jeffrey made a sound of disbelief as he considered the grainy picture someone had taken of him leaving the lab facility where he worked.

"This is…" The second page derailed whatever he'd planned to say next.

The second page listed his name, address, occupation and a full physical description.

"What the hell is this, Olivia?"

She checked to ensure the doors were locked and pressed more firmly on the accelerator. She doubted he would attempt to escape the vehicle with her going eighty miles per hour, but she didn't want to risk it. People reacted differently to extreme stress or fear. A perfectly intelligent man might turn irrational.

"Someone has ordered a hit on you, Jeffrey. Maybe someone from a competing facility." She suggested the latter to lend more credibility to the statement. She remained doubtful that this was about him…more likely it was about who she used to be. But for now, both scenarios were still on the table.

Either way, this had something to do with her past. The only question in her mind was the motive. Why would anyone want to wake the dead now? After three years? It wasn't as if she'd walked away with any secrets or intelligence that would benefit anyone in the spy business these days.

Still, her Sheara cover had not been reactivated for no reason. The idea that Ned Soderbaum didn't exist and that he'd used an old enemy as his source indicated that the impetus ran deep, all the way back to the Agency.

And the Phantom.

The muscles of her face and neck instantly tightened. Even if he'd known she was still alive, why would he blow her new identity? It made no sense. She had nothing he wanted. He'd made that clear when he walked away leaving her with no one to back up her story. Leaving her to face a possible murder charge.

Deputy Director Hamilton was the only reason she had escaped that fate. Her former boss was the reason she had to get to Virginia ASAP.

"Olivia, this is no longer the slightest bit amusing or intriguing." Jeffrey's voice intruded into her disturbing thoughts. "Either you're playing one hell of a bad joke on me or you're empathizing with one or more of your patients a little too well. I'm really worried here."

She tightened her fingers on the steering wheel and took the only option she had at the moment. "I'm sorry you're worried. But you have to trust me on this, Jeffrey. We have to do this my way."

He reached into his shirt pocket and pulled out his cell phone. "I'm certain you believe every word you've told me, but you're not thinking rationally. Clearly you're not yourself. We need assistance."

Oh, hell. She'd run out of options. Olivia seized the weapon from her bag and pointed the business end in his general direction. She really hated to do this, but… "Put the phone in my bag, Jeffrey. Don't ask any more questions. We'll be in Memphis soon and then we'll discuss the situation." He didn't have to know there wasn't even a round in the chamber.

"Have you lost your mind? Put that thing away!"

So much for pulling off her former persona. If she couldn't put the fear of God in Jeffrey, she was pretty much screwed.

She shoved the gun back into her bag. She wasn't worried about Jeffrey attempting to grab it. He knew absolutely nothing about weapons.

"Let's just not argue, okay?" She looked at him for as long as she dared with her speed hanging around eighty. "I have to do this. Can't that be enough for now?"

The hesitation before he nodded had her holding her breath. "All right. We'll figure this out when we get to Memphis."

"Thank you." His agreement most likely had more

to do with his fear that she'd lost her mind completely than anything else, but she'd take it any way it came. She inhaled deeply and let the breath go, her mind and body weary. Four, maybe five more hours. She could hold out that long. It had been years since she'd pushed her body to perform without sleep. If she was lucky that was another old habit that would be easy to fall back into.

Contacting Hamilton was her only chance at getting to the bottom of whatever the hell was going on. If he couldn't help her, then she was on her on.

Pulling off the interstate at a chain hotel just west of Memphis, Olivia finally let her body sag with relief. It was past 6:00 a.m. She'd been driving for twenty-four hours straight, only stopping for gas and bathroom breaks. She'd eaten a sandwich behind the wheel and she felt starved now, but that would have to wait. She needed sleep far more than food.

Jeffrey stretched as best he could in the seat as she parked in front of the hotel's office. "I can take care of the room if you like."

Under normal circumstances she would know that he was being considerate, but these circumstances were anything but normal. She couldn't risk that he wanted an opportunity to call for help. He had unquestionably decided that she'd flipped out. If she were him, she'd likely think the same thing.

"That's all right. I'll get it."

Still trusting of her despite her recent behavior, he didn't have time to fathom her intent before it was too late, when she took his left hand.

She snapped the cuff into place, then fastened the matching one to the steering wheel.

"I'll be right back."

He jerked at the restraint. "Olivia! This is unconscionable! How could—"

"I'll be right back," she reiterated before grabbing her handbag and sliding out of the SUV. She was too damn tired to try to make him understand.

She didn't bother looking back as she entered the lobby. She had his cell and, thankfully, Explorers weren't equipped with anything like OnStar, so he wasn't going to be making any calls. They hadn't been followed, so she wasn't worried about his safety.

"Good morning, ma'am." The clerk offered her a smile, no matter that his shift was likely nearly at an end and he probably wanted to sleep as badly as she did.

"Morning. I'd like a room. Nonsmoking, two double beds, on the ground floor, please."

He pecked a few keys on the computer keyboard. "Nothing like a lady who knows what she wants." His smile widened to a grin. "That's why I like my job. It's always interesting."

He had no idea. "And a wake-up call," she added as she placed her credit card on the counter.

"Gotcha." He swiped her card. Handed it back to

her along with a key card for the room. "What time you wanna get up, ma'am?"

"Ten."

His eyebrows shot up. "A.m.?"

"Yes, please."

"Lady, it's six-thirty now. You wanna get up in three and a half hours?"

The young man had his mathematics down pat—too bad he couldn't keep a handle on his professionalism. "Yes, that's correct."

His shoulders rose and fell. "Whatever floats your boat." A few more key clicks. "You're set."

"Thank you."

She could feel the man watching her as she exited the lobby, but she didn't worry about that. Working a hotel on the interstate ensured that he saw more than his fair share of weary travelers. Long-distance travelers were usually in a hurry to get to their destinations: he wouldn't be that surprised at her request. His reaction had more to do with flirting than anything else.

Olivia shook off the psychologist persona and zeroed in on her hostage, of sorts. He glared at her. It was plenty light enough for her to see that from quite a distance.

"Sorry about this, Jeffrey," she offered as she released him.

He jerked his hand away once it was free of its metal bracelet. "I cannot believe you just did that." His profile was set in stone, so unlike the man she knew so well. "I've been very forgiving so far, but I'm not so sure I'll be able to forgive this brutal act."

He so did not know the meaning of the word *brutal*.

"I understand."

Why argue? It wouldn't accomplish anything and she was too damn tired to really care what he thought at the moment. Unfortunately for him it was only going to get worse from here.

She drove around to the rear of the hotel, spotting their unit number near the middle of the building. She backed into the parking spot directly in front of the door, grabbed her handbag and got out.

Her passenger climbed out on the opposite side and, to his credit, he didn't make a run for it. Rather, he took their two overnight bags from the cargo area and transported them into the room. She appreciated his gentlemanly act, which left her the Neiman Marcus bag to grab.

"Two beds?" He stared at her, confusion joining the mixture of other emotions currently cluttering his face when they'd entered the room.

"I wasn't sure you'd feel comfortable sleeping with me under the circumstances."

He dropped the bags near the chair and table on the east side of the room. "You have a point." He kicked off his shoes and sat down on the end of the bed closest to the door. He studied her with mounting concern. "Make me understand what's going on, Olivia. I'm worried about you."

Olivia placed the shopping bag, as well as her purse, on the floor next to her bed, then sat down. She untied her hiking boots and toed them off.

For several minutes they both sat there, physically depleted and mentally distressed. There were so many aspects of this situation that she didn't understand. None of it really made sense. She could imagine that it was even more confusing and shocking to Jeffrey. How did she make him understand what was happening when she wasn't even sure?

"Olivia, please tell me what's happened. You must know that I'll try my best to understand and that I'll help any way possible." A small humorless laugh choked out of him. "Despite the fact that you pointed a gun at me. Handcuffed me, for Christ's sake. But I care about you. Otherwise I'd be out of here instead of hanging around asking for more. Let me help you," he urged.

Every word he said was true. No matter how shocking her actions, he wouldn't dare leave her alone. He might try to call for help—for her—but he'd never abandon her, especially in a time of obvious distress. Unlike the last man with whom she'd shared a relationship.

She wanted to reassure Jeffrey by saying that everything was fine, but she wasn't sure it ever would be again. She didn't like doing this to him any more than he liked her doing it. Not that she was really in love with him...she wasn't. She wasn't sure she could love anyone. Not after...well, she wasn't going there.

But she did care about Jeffrey. He was comfortable. Reliable. Familiar. Like a favorite old bathrobe. She knew exactly what to expect out of him. He was safe. She liked safe. Her current life was all about careful and...to be honest...boring. Boring was better than dangerous. She'd faced enough danger to last a dozen lifetimes.

"Jeffrey, everything I told you is the truth. There are things about my past that I can't disclose, but you have to believe that I wouldn't lie to you about anything like this."

He scooted back on his bed and lay against the pillows, whether to put some distance between them or just to relax she couldn't be sure. "I don't think you're lying. I hesitate to go so far as to call what I've witnessed in the past twenty-four hours delusional, but you must admit that it feels exactly like that...as if you've crossed some boundary. Are you certain there isn't some stressor your mind is attempting to escape?"

There were stressors her mind wanted to escape rightly enough, but he was wrong on all other counts. How did she make a civilian understand how things worked in the world that had once been her life?

She didn't. It was as simple as that. There were reasons that security measures were doled out on a need-to-know basis. In this instance, Jeffrey didn't need to know any more than absolutely necessary to ensure his continued cooperation.

"You're right, Jeffrey." Might as well play along. Anything to get him to remain calm. "I've suffered a traumatic event. The man I'm going to see in Virginia is involved. I need to see this through."

"Virginia?" A new kind of shock claimed his expression. "We're going to Virginia?"

"We don't have a choice." Olivia curled up against her own pillows and met his gaze. "I need you to understand that my continued well-being hinges upon doing this. I need to be able to count on you."

His gaze narrowed slightly. "Then what about the picture of me and the personal information? Are you saying you made that part up?"

She shook her head. "I believe that someone wants to hurt me and they're trying to use you to get to me. It's complicated. And dangerous."

"I see." He searched her eyes as if looking for any glimmer of deceit. His own reflected his worry, his need to take care of her. "You don't think calling the authorities would be the best way to take care of this situation?"

"I have to do this myself. It's very important."

She hated this. Hated using his loyalty to what they'd shared these past nine months. Lies, lies, lies. She'd thought she was through with that way of life. The reality that she wasn't churned in her stomach.

"We should try to sleep." He yawned, gave her a reassuring smile. "We'll be able to think more clearly when we've rested. Whatever this is about, we'll work it out."

When his breathing had slowed to a deep, steady rhythm, she finally let herself relax fully. She wasn't worried about him trying to run out on her. Like he said, he cared. He wouldn't leave her.

How the hell had this happened? Now, after all this time?

She flopped onto her back and tried to reason out some part—any part—of this situation. There was no rhyme or reason to it.

For the first time since the insanity began she let herself think about him…the Phantom. *Holt Landry*. She closed her eyes and permitted the memories she'd kept tightly compartmentalized to rush over her.

They'd met on an assignment just over five years ago. A joint CIA/Interpol operation. She'd been charmed. He'd been relentless. They'd become lovers almost immediately. For two years they'd had an intense physical relationship. Like a fool, she'd fallen in love with him. She hadn't planned it; it simply happened.

She and Landry hadn't lived together as she and Jeffrey did, but their relationship had been far more powerful. On fire. She'd felt disconnected when separated from him, which was quite frequently.

Somehow he'd always made it worth her while when they were together again. No one had ever made love to her the way Landry had.

Damn him.

Those damn muscles in her face hardened again, clenching her teeth in a way that threatened to damage the enamel.

He'd stolen her heart and then he'd walked away when she needed him most.

Those last days after her final assignment came pouring into the thoughts already disturbing her sanity. She'd killed an innocent man. But he'd been her target! She'd had orders. Orders Landry could have confirmed when the Agency denied the operation.

Instead, Landry had disappeared, leaving her to face the consequences alone. She hadn't done anything wrong. Followed orders, that was all. CIA-sanctioned orders. But she couldn't prove it. She'd been the scapegoat for whoever had decided the target needed to die. End of story.

If it hadn't been for her faithful friend and deputy director, she would have gone to prison, or worse. Rogue agents disappeared quite frequently. Quietly terminated to ensure the world never learned their secrets.

But Hamilton had taken care of her. He'd faked her death and convinced all involved that she was indeed dead. No one had ever come looking for her…until now.

To her knowledge, Hamilton was the only person on Earth who knew that she was alive.

Had he betrayed her? For what reason? And why use Jeffrey to lure her out of hiding? If he knew where she was, why set up such an unnecessary ruse?

Even Hamilton hadn't known her new identity or her location. He'd wanted it that way. She'd set up her new life. No one she'd ever associated with or ever known had been in on it. She'd walked away from everything and everyone.

Hamilton was her only connection to the past. Had he sold her out to Landry?

That theory didn't seem reasonable. There was nothing to gain. Even the CIA's top brass wouldn't likely care if they learned she was alive at this point. The political repercussions of her actions three years ago had gone out with the former White House administration. No one in the new administration would give a damn, as far as she could see.

Olivia pushed the troubling thoughts out of her head. She had to sleep. She still had a long way to go.

Staying on her toes was absolutely necessary if she wanted to survive this. And there was no way she would allow Jeffrey to be used as a pawn. He was innocent…had nothing to do with her past. Whoever was behind this little reunion would not be allowed to harm him. She couldn't rule out the idea that someone might have targeted him, but the likelihood of her being chosen as the assassin in that case was so remote, so damn coincidental, she had a hard time lending any merit at all to the idea.

She would have her answers.

All she had to do was get to Hamilton. He had full access…he would know what to do.

Slipping past his security wouldn't be easy, especially for someone as out of practice as she was. But since when had she been afraid of six or seven guys with guns? Determination fired inside her.

Since never.

She was Sheara, Goddess of Death. She wasn't afraid of anyone.

All she had to do was remember that.

Chapter 5

"I refuse to take another step."

Olivia shoved her night-vision goggles up to her forehead and turned to glare at the man behind her. Not that he would notice. It was past midnight and darker than a cave in these damn woods.

"You're right." She moved a step in his direction. The tension roiling through him was audible in his words as well as his ragged respiration. He'd long ago lost patience. Now panic had begun to set in. He wanted to be angry, Olivia sensed, but his concern for her kept his emotions bogged down in escalating anxiety. She was lucky he'd come this far with her.

"You've been extremely flexible about this whole thing, Jeffrey, and I appreciate it immensely. You've made what I have to do a lot easier so far. At this point, though, there are additional risks involved in what I'm about to do. It would probably be in your best interest to stay here, clear of any fallout."

"Wait a minute…" He reached for her, his movement barely visible in the sparse moonlight filtering down through the dense canopy of trees. "What is it you're going to do, Olivia? You've been far too vague about your plans. I don't understand any of this. I've told you repeatedly that not going to the authorities is a mistake." His fingers closed around her arms and he pulled her closer. "I can see that this situation has you terrified, but reacting rashly won't solve the problem. There are laws to protect the innocent. Those same laws prosecute those who threaten us." A breath of frustration and worry heaved out of him. "We're out here in the dark, traipsing through the woods. What could you possibly hope to gain by doing this?"

She was reasonably certain he wouldn't want to know the truth. But giving him some fraction of the truth might keep him following her orders. He'd left the hotel in Memphis without much of a fuss. Had remained amicable during the long drive that followed. She couldn't call him unreasonable at this point. They'd left the SUV hidden in the bushes well off the road and started their trek through the woods about an hour ago, and even faced with that strange request he hadn't complained much.

How could she expect any more of him?

She couldn't.

"About fifteen minutes west of our current position there's a farm," she explained. "The owner of that farm is the man I need to see." Director Hamilton had always spent his weekends at his farm a couple of hours outside Arlington. It was where he decompressed and contemplated the many decisions he had to make during the workweek at the Agency. He would be here tonight, there wasn't a doubt in Olivia's mind. But security would be there, as well. Bypassing them wouldn't be a problem for her, but Jeffrey was a different matter.

She'd been waiting for the right moment to break the news to him. He would stay back and she would move on, do what she had to do, then return for him. It was the best course of action.

"You expect me to stay here while you go have your meeting? Alone? Olivia, have you lost your mind? Why didn't we just drive to this farm? Surely there's access from the main road. I'm not letting you do this alone."

A new kind of determination had edged into his voice.

Maybe she had lost her mind. But she didn't really have any better ideas at the moment. And she couldn't let him get in the way...too much was at stake, including his life.

"I need the element of surprise on my side, Jeffrey. That's all I can tell you. I'll be fine. I've done this before."

"When have you done this before?" Exasperation overtook some of the determination. "This is—"

She fisted her fingers into his shirtfront. "Jeffrey, you have to trust me. I swear I know what I'm doing. If you don't let me get this done…" She licked her lips, tried to think of some rational reason he might accept. "I'll be in very serious trouble. Please trust me on this."

Another lungful of frustration burst from him. "I swear this is my final compromise. I'll wait here, but you'd better hurry back. If this situation isn't resolved after this, we're going to the authorities. No negotiation."

She could live with that. For now. "Okay." She tugged the .32 from her waistband, then turned on the flashlight long enough to give him a quick block of instruction in the gun's use. "Just stay in the bushes and keep quiet."

"You know how I feel about guns."

"I'll feel a lot better if you take these." She held out the gun and the flashlight.

A beat of silence passed before he relented. "Don't worry about me." His fingers closed reluctantly around the butt of the weapon and he took it from her. He accepted the flashlight a little more readily. "I can take care of myself. You're the one I'm worried about."

"Don't use your phone unless you have no other choice. If you call the authorities, Jeffrey, my situation could be compromised." She'd given back his

BlackBerry as a sign of good faith when he'd agreed to make the rest of the trip with her.

"I won't call anyone unless absolutely necessary." Another disinclined conciliation.

Olivia considered what might happen if she didn't return. "It's one-fifteen. If I'm not back by three, I want you to make your way back to the SUV and disappear for a while. Take a vacation somewhere. Just don't go back to California for the next week or so." She wasn't completely certain he would be safe even then, but it was the best advice she could offer at this point.

He made a sound that might have been a laugh had it not been chock-full of worry. "If you're not back soon, I'm going to the police."

She supposed she couldn't expect to control his actions if she didn't return. She could only offer her best advice. There simply was no way to make him fully understand the situation. The concept was too foreign for a normal person's mind to wrap around.

Nothing would ever be the same from this moment forward. Jeffrey still believed in her, cared about her, wanted to protect her. But once he knew the whole truth, any feelings he had for her would disappear like so much smoke in the wind. Regret trickled through her. Once again her life had been taken away from her. Ripped from her as if she was so insignificant that her feelings—her happiness— didn't matter.

"I'll be back as quickly as possible."

She disappeared into the dense woods without

saying more. Anything else would only make what she knew came next more difficult. Jeffrey didn't deserve to have his life at risk. It was her problem.

If she didn't make it out, Jeffrey might never be safe again—depending upon what the enemy wanted. No one deserved to die for someone else's sins.

Determination roared through her. That settled it then. She'd just have to get through this and make sure Jeffrey didn't pay for her transgressions.

Deputy Director David Hamilton's log home, nestled amid the soaring evergreens and hardwoods of the Virginia countryside, presented the perfect Norman Rockwell setting. Serene, natural and welcoming. But she knew better than to be fooled by the lovely picture spotlighted in its meticulously landscaped clearing by the low-slung moon.

Bulletproof windows. Half a dozen armed security guards. Motion sensors. Maybe even a few booby traps.

A walk in the park for Sheara. But Olivia hadn't played this game in a long time. Stepping on an unexpected "boom" rig or stumbling over a trip wire that would warn security of her presence held no appeal whatsoever.

With her Beretta tucked in her waistband and the hunting knife sheathed in her right hiking boot, she slowly slipped into stealth mode. Her movements were a little stilted at first. She made more noise than she would have liked. So she took her time breaching the boundary into the clearing. No need to rush. She had to get her groove back.

She held her breath as she took the first step. When no explosion sounded and the pounding of booted feet didn't echo nearby, she figured she'd cleared the first hurdle.

She hunkered down behind a cluster of shrubs as two guards emerged from the shadows at the far corner of the house. Rounds. She checked her watch. Probably made on the half hour. There would likely be two more in the house and perhaps an additional one or two making rounds in the woods that bordered the clearing. Since she hadn't encountered security inside the treeline she had to assume that the rounds were alternated, or maybe she'd gotten lucky and they'd been on the west side of the property as she approached from the east.

Okay. There was no going in at this point without being made and that could prove hazardous to her health.

That left only one other option. She needed a "pass go" authorization. Only one way to get her hands on that kind of access.

She eased back into the woods and waited. Fifteen minutes, she estimated. The outer-boundary scout or scouts should move through her area within fifteen minutes. Thirty tops. She hated to waste the time but better to be safe than sorry.

Fourteen minutes and thirty seconds later and the soft crunch of footsteps crackled through the darkness.

Perfect timing.

Anticipation fired through her veins, the adrenaline burning her insides. Her heart rate accelerated into a fight-or-flight rhythm.

If there were two, the job would be a little trickier.

With her night-vision goggles in place, she watched the approach. One man. Her pulse reacted to the upturn in her luck. There could still be another one out there, but taking them out one at a time would greatly increase her odds of success.

He passed not three feet from her and she was ready. She lunged into his back, her right arm going around his throat, her left hand over his mouth. He struggled. He was strong. But she was desperate. Adrenaline won out.

The guy dropped to his knees. Not taking any chances, Olivia blocked his airflow a few seconds longer to ensure he'd truly lost consciousness. He crumpled against her and she lowered him to the ground. Her intent had not been to kill him, only to disable him. He'd regain consciousness pretty quickly, so she had to work fast.

She stripped off his clothes, dragged them on over her own, including the black skull cap. She left him naked and unarmed on the ground, his hands cuffed behind his back. Her belt fastened behind his head with the wide leather strap tucked between his teeth gag style.

After surveying the clearing, she stepped from the cover of the woods. She walked straight up to the generous front porch and climbed the steps. She'd found a key card in the guard's pocket. One look at the front door and she knew what it was used for. She swiped the card and entered the house. Just like a hotel room. Shame on the director. He, of all people, should have retinal- or fingerprint-scan requirements. He had to be getting soft.

The entry hall was dimly lit. She was surprised to find herself seemingly alone inside. Maybe her luck was going to hold out.

Her steps silent, she'd made it halfway to the staircase when the unmistakable feel of a muzzle nudged the back of her skull.

"Don't move."

Her hands went up in classic surrender fashion. Damn. She hadn't even heard him coming. "I'm here to see Director Hamilton."

The guard's radio crackled and he responded. "I have the intruder."

He patted her down, removed the Beretta and the knife, then the guard's .45 she'd taken.

"On the floor."

"I said I'm here to see the director."

"The director isn't home."

Olivia held her ground. "You tell him Sheara needs to see him."

"I told you—"

"That'll be all, Smith."

Olivia's head went up. Deputy Director David Hamilton stood at the top of the staircase, a dim light from somewhere beyond him highlighting his silhouette.

"Sir, she came in heavily armed, used Bedwell's key card."

"I said, that'll be all, Smith."

Retreating footsteps told Olivia the guard had moved away from her. She slowly lowered her hands.

Hamilton didn't really look that different. A little older and thinner maybe. More gray hair. Nothing significant. He actually looked pretty damn good for a man closer to sixty than fifty. He wore an elegant robe over comfortable-looking pajamas. He'd taken the time to put on house slippers and smooth his hair before leaving his room. Hamilton was never one to be caught with his trousers down. He probably had a weapon somewhere on his person. Maybe two.

"Hello, Vanessa."

The chill of danger, however familiar, whispered through her. *Vanessa.* That had been her name before. The name she'd been given at birth. Vanessa Clark.

"Hamilton," she acknowledged, instinctively moving to a posture of full attention.

His hands tucked casually into the pockets of his robe, he descended a couple of steps. "The key card you used is biometrics, new technology. The card itself recognizes the fingerprints of the carrier. Though it allowed you access, it also sent a warning to the head of security."

"Interesting." She should have known he'd have that base covered.

"I assume you have a good reason for breaking cover."

"I didn't break cover." She suddenly felt like a recruit facing her instructor after having made a stupid mistake in training. "My code name was re-activated."

Two more steps disappeared behind him. "Someone activated Sheara?" He sounded sincerely surprised.

"That's right."

The frown that furrowed his brow looked genuine enough. "I sunk that code name along with your last assignment and complete personnel file when you died."

"Yeah, well, someone resurrected me."

He paused, eight treads up from her position. His right hand moved from his pocket to caress his chin thoughtfully. She'd watched him do that a million times. The familiarity felt almost surreal.

"No one at the Agency, I'm certain."

Two more steps down.

"No one else knew I was alive." Her pulse slammed wildly. He understood that she'd just openly accused him: the apprehension was right there in those wise gray eyes.

"Absolutely no one," he agreed. "I personally made sure of that."

She angled her head to stare directly up at him. "How do you suppose this happened?"

He moved down the final step. "That's what we're going to find out."

Profound relief gushed through Olivia. She'd felt as if she was in this all alone when that call had come. She'd relied heavily on the idea that she could count on Hamilton. Thankfully her instincts had been right.

"You look exhausted. How about some coffee?"

"I could use the caffeine."

It was 2:00 a.m. when Olivia sat down at the deputy director's kitchen table and watched him prepare a pot of imported coffee. His taste had always run to the exotic. He rambled on about the post–9/11 changes in the Agency. He despised reporting to a higher administration. In his opinion the nuisance was not only a waste of time but debilitating on numerous levels.

Olivia had known when she'd read about the shake-up in the federal agencies that Hamilton wouldn't approve. But it was a different world now—change was inevitable.

When he joined her at the table with two cups of steaming black coffee, she gave him the rest of the story, including the one piece of evidence she had on who might be behind her unwanted resurrection: the Phantom.

"I didn't realize he was still around. He certainly hasn't worked any joint operations with us since that last assignment he coordinated with you."

"Don't remind me," she muttered as she sipped her coffee. The warm brew soothed as it slid down her throat, the robust flavor promising a serious caffeine kick.

"The way I see it," Hamilton began, "you and your friend should disappear until we've cleared this up. I'll conduct my own under-the-table investigation. Make sure this didn't somehow come from us, though I'm very doubtful of that possibility."

So was Olivia. She didn't know how the Phantom had found her and she sure as hell couldn't imagine what he wanted. Maybe to finish the job of ruining her? Apparently the fact that he'd played a large part in ending her career three years ago wasn't quite enough. She said as much to Director Hamilton.

He rubbed his chin again, those analyzing wheels turning in his head. "I'm not so sure it's as simple as that, Vanessa."

She didn't bother correcting him. He didn't know her new name, there was no reason for him to. "Why do you say that?"

"What would he have to gain? We both know Landry. It isn't as if he would launch an operation, official or unofficial, without some sort of motivation. There has to be a reason. A goal. Andrew Page, his superior, is a good man. I can't see either of them being the culprit now or then."

She resisted the urge to touch the small gold heart…the only connection she'd kept to her old life besides the old cell number. She wasn't afraid of the necklace. She'd checked it out. No tracking device, no bugs. Obviously he'd known her location before he'd had some jerk call her old Sheara number, otherwise he wouldn't have known about Jeffrey, but he hadn't learned it from the necklace.

She blinked, remembering that Jeffrey was waiting for her to return.

"I should go." She stood before she could change her mind.

"You're welcome to stay the night, Vanessa." Hamilton rose from his chair, his movements a little slower than she remembered. "Get some sleep. Let me check into this. I'll get you and your friend to a safe house."

She shook her head. "You do your thing and I'll be in touch. Is there a secure line I can use to contact you?"

He rattled off a number and she entered it into the address book of her cell.

When she would have walked away, he drew her attention once more. "Stay under the radar, Vanessa. Whoever started this could be an extremely dangerous enemy."

She let him have a good long look at the determination she felt before she spoke. "So can I."

"Touché." He laughed softly. "I wouldn't want to lay odds on either side, especially if Landry is the one. Just give me twenty-four hours to ensure that the Agency or Interpol isn't up to something we don't know about. There may be a legitimate reason he's drawing you out."

She doubted that, but she had no proof either way. "Twenty-four hours."

This time she got all the way to the front door when the guard named Smith stopped her. "The clothes." He gestured to the garb she wore over her own.

"No problem." She stripped off the uniform she'd borrowed. As tired as she was, it gave her immense pleasure to watch Smith's indifference turn to interest, then disappointment, as her fully attired body was revealed beneath the baggy uniform.

She tossed the bundle at him and left. "My weapons." He returned her Beretta and the knife. She tucked both away, noted the time and hoped Jeffrey hadn't started to get nervous. If she moved quickly enough she could be back at his position in twelve or thirteen minutes.

Jeffrey had just checked his watch and heaved a worried sigh when she reached him.

"I'm back," she announced.

He whipped around at the sound of her voice, gun drawn, and she was enormously grateful he didn't fire off a round. Maybe she should have warned him of her approach a little sooner.

"Are you all right?"

He looked agitated and very pale, even in the near-total darkness. He had been worried, worried sick. Guilt weighed heavy on her shoulders.

"I'm fine. Let's get out of here."

"Did you find the man you needed to see?"

"Yes."

"What did he say?"

Olivia kept walking, assuming he would follow. "Nothing I didn't already know."

"So what does that mean? What do we do now? Is it safe to go back to L.A.?"

Waiting until they were in the SUV and on their way to tell him what came next was totally necessary. If she told him now, she'd likely be out here until daylight convincing him to go along with her plan.

So she did what she'd always done best, at least up until three years ago. She lied.

"Yeah, we can go home now."

"Thank God. I still think you should have the authorities look into this. This has been a nightmare for you. You can't just let it go."

"You're right," she agreed solemnly. "I can't let him get away with this."

And that, she reiterated silently, was the truth.

Chapter 6

The entire journey back to the Explorer, Jeffrey remained silent and stayed very close to her. Olivia was pretty sure he was afraid that she might launch into some other strange behavior and wanted to be prepared to restrain her. Or maybe he was just so happy with the prospect of going home that he didn't dare speak for fear she'd change her mind.

She'd known Jeffrey nine months now and not once had she considered what he would think about her old life. Strange. So much of her life had been spent in covert operations, climbing mountains, hunkering down in jungles, watching a target through a scope. She'd known, of course, that she could never tell him because he surely wouldn't understand. But she hadn't considered what he would think if she *had* to tell him for one reason or the other.

She'd never expected to have to tell him.

When they reached the copse of trees and bushes where she'd parked the SUV, she stopped. Something felt wrong.

"What is it now?" He moved up right behind her, close enough that she could feel the heat of his body.

"Let's just listen a moment."

It was still dark but she found herself doing a three-sixty as she peered into the night. The special night-vision goggles helped but not as well as a nice ray of sunshine would have.

Nothing moved. No sign of warm-blooded creatures, human or otherwise, in the area.

Yet she had the overwhelming sensation that something was out of sync.

"You think someone is watching us?" Jeffrey spoke quietly, as if he understood the need for caution just now.

"I don't know."

Her instincts nudged at her but she couldn't pinpoint precisely what the problem was. She tugged off her night vision and climbed into the vehicle. Jeffrey slid into the passenger seat, his own instincts on alert now.

She started the engine, the very hair on the back of her neck standing on end. Something was definitely wrong.

"Can you tell me how it went back there?" Jeffrey

snapped his seat belt into place. "You said you didn't learn anything you didn't already know."

"It was a very productive meeting in some ways." She pulled the gearshift into Reverse and backed out onto the highway. She braced for his reaction to what she had to do next. Shifting into Drive, she roared forward, needing to put as much distance as possible between her and Hamilton. Not that she didn't trust Hamilton—she did. At least as much as any player could trust another. There was always the risk that he would double-cross her for reasons unknown to her. The greater good. In this business it was all relative. It was nothing personal.

"Since we're both been dragged into this," Jeffrey ventured, apparently set on having more information, "I should know what exactly that means. It's inconsiderate of you to keep me in the dark like this. I understand the concept of privilege, but there are clearly extenuating circumstances here."

"That's a good idea, Olivia. Let's not keep the man in the dark."

Deep, smooth and rich like the finest Merlot. *His* voice.

The recognition crashed into her like a 747 dropping from the sky. Her gaze shot to the rearview mirror at the same instant that her right foot slammed on the brake.

The Phantom.

"Who the hell are you?" Jeffrey demanded.

If the man in the backseat answered him Olivia didn't hear it. She was a little busy.

The SUV slid sideways. She struggled to right it. How the hell had he found her?

When the vehicle was parallel with the road once more, she cut sharply to the right and bounced onto the shoulder. Jeffrey shouted for her to be careful but she ignored him. Ramming the gearshift into Park with her right hand, she wrenched her door open with her left and jumped out of the vehicle.

The back door flew open and Landry was on his feet, but she had a bead right between his arrogant eyes before he could straighten to his full height.

"Well, well. Looks like we have ourselves a small dilemma," Landry said.

The SUV's interior light was dim but not so much so that she couldn't see the Glock in his hand as he stepped beyond his open door. He'd always favored that family of weapons.

"What do you want, Landry?" Her heart thudded unmercifully against the wall of her chest and breathing was practically impossible. She told herself it had nothing to do with those devastating blue eyes or those perfectly formed lips. No man should be allowed to look this good. She wanted to hurt him—no—she wanted to *kill* him. For three years ago…for now.

"Olivia? Who is this man?"

Dammit. Jeffrey made his way around the hood of the SUV and came up behind her. Why hadn't he stayed in the car?

"What do you want?" Jeffrey demanded before she could answer his first question.

The smile that cut across Landry's face at the question made her want to slug him.

"This is a private conversation, *Jeffrey*." Landry made the smug remark without taking his eyes off her, allowing her no window of opportunity to make a move. "You should get back in the vehicle before you get hurt," he tacked on as if he gave one shit what happened to an innocent bystander.

"Olivia, we should call the police—"

"Get in the car," she urged. "I'll explain everything in a minute."

Her fingers tightened on her weapon. Instinct had taken over when she'd jumped out of the SUV, ensuring that she adopted a firing stance. It would be so easy…but then Landry would shoot and if he survived and she didn't he would kill Jeffrey just to tie up any loose ends.

"We have two choices, Nessa—"

"Don't call me that." Something on the order of hatred seared through her veins. It was all she could do not to squeeze the trigger. That he would intrude into her life again after what he did made her crazy angry. But the other thing—those stupid, sentimental feelings of yearning that somehow awoke from the dead the instant she heard his voice—wouldn't allow her to pull that trigger.

Jeffrey sidled up a little closer to her. "Olivia, do you really know how to use that weapon?"

"Get in the goddamn car, Jeffrey, before you get us both killed." When he still hesitated, she pressed, "Please, Jeffrey."

The sound of his hiking boots wading through the ankle-deep grass and then the door slamming on the passenger side of the vehicle signaled that he had deferred to her wishes without her having to look away from the enemy.

"As I was saying." Landry leaned against the open door, his aim steady. "We have two choices. We can either kill each other or we can figure out who the hell started this thing and do something about it."

Fury exploded inside her, bigger, harder than before. How dare he! "I already know who started this, you bastard. You did!"

There went any chance of remaining calm.

His gaze narrowed, which was his only visible concession to whatever was on his mind. "You think I started this?"

Disbelief joined the fury. "You gave that creep Soderbaum or whoever the hell he was my number. My code name. *You* started this."

"Someone activated your code name?"

What was he up to? "You know that's why I'm here. That's why *you're* here. Soderbaum approached me about a target."

"What target? Who is this Soderbaum you keep talking about?"

Olivia blinked, suddenly unsure of how she should proceed. Some rogue part of her wanted desperately to believe Landry wasn't the one—that betraying her once had been more than enough. "Soderbaum, the client who contacted Sheara, wanted Jeffrey eliminated. He said you were his reference."

"We've been set up."

Yeah, right. "Like I'd believe anything you said. Just tell me what you want and let's get this over with, shall we?"

He shook his head. "We've been had, Vanessa. We were both drawn out for a reason. I came here because I got an anonymous tip that you'd be here."

It was her turn to shake her head. "Do you really think I believe that crap? You betrayed me once, Landry. I won't be falling for any of your lies this time."

"That's something else we fail to agree upon." He surveyed the deserted highway, giving her ample opportunity and showing once and for all that she was an even bigger fool than she'd thought when she didn't shoot him dead. "Let's just get in the vehicle and get out of here. We can talk about this when we're not sitting ducks."

Maybe it was the dim moonlight, but she would swear he suddenly looked nervous. Then again, she would cling to almost any hope that might disprove her own stupidity.

"You get in first." She wasn't about to turn her back on Landry.

But there wasn't really any choice just now.

Two seconds of thickening silence passed. "Fine."

He shoved the Glock into his waistband and climbed into the backseat.

Olivia stood there for three or four more seconds before she could move. Her legs felt rubbery when she did. She slid behind the wheel and shifted into Drive. She dispatched Jeffrey a look that left no question as to exactly how serious she was. "Don't ask any questions right now. I'll explain everything later."

Evidently stunned speechless, he remained silent as she drove back the way they had come. She needed a plan. She'd intended to form one. But now, with *him* in the backseat, she couldn't think.

How had he followed her here? Anonymous tip. Bull. He had to be the one who'd set this game in motion. Of course he'd know she'd come to Hamilton. That was exactly how he'd ambushed her. Her former boss was her only option for support. The reason for his decision to ruin her life all over again wasn't so easy to deduce. Only *he* could answer that one.

Her teeth gritted together, her fingers fisted on the steering wheel. Holt Landry was right behind her, barely two feet away. Another wave of anger erupted to the surface. Why wasn't he off playing James Bond somewhere? Why did he have to come barging into her life again? What did he want?

And why the hell had she turned her back on him? She'd sworn she wouldn't and here she was with him right behind her.

The questions pounded away at her brain, making her want to scream.

"We have a tail."

She glanced in the rearview mirror. Headlights glowed in the distance.

"How long has he been following us?"

"He showed up right after you took off."

She definitely should have noticed him before Landry did. A perfect example of how easily he distracted her. Stupid, stupid, stupid.

She studied the headlights reflected in the rearview mirror. It was four o'clock in the morning. She supposed it wasn't totally impossible that someone would be on this desolate back road at that time of day, but she wasn't about to chance it. Her foot pressed harder on the accelerator. The Explorer rocketed forward taking the curves in the road far too fast. The other vehicle did the same.

Oh, yeah, definitely a tail.

The headlights bobbed closer.

She bit her bottom lip. Could she outrun him?

The Explorer went off the edge of the pavement and bumped along the shoulder. Olivia's heart lunged into her throat. She fought to right her mistake. With one careful cut of the steering wheel the SUV jerked back onto the pavement. She didn't take another breath until the vehicle had stopped swaying and she had regained the speed she'd lost.

"You keep your eyes on the road," Landry ordered. "I'll take care of the tail."

Jeffrey leaned forward, both hands braced

against the dash. "Olivia, are you sure you know what you're doing?"

Hell, no rushed to the tip of her tongue but she bit it back. "Yes." The single word sounded damn hollow and utterly unconvincing but Jeffrey didn't argue. He no doubt understood that this was very bad.

The headlights bore down on her. The other vehicle was practically on her bumper now.

"You're going to have to move a little faster."

The urgency in Landry's tone sent adrenaline charging through her limbs. If he was worried, they were in real trouble. She floored the accelerator, kept it there.

"Oh, God!" Jeffrey pressed back against the seat.

She saw it coming and still Olivia wasn't prepared for the impact. The other vehicle whipped into the left lane and rushed up next to her only to slam sideways into her. The Explorer lurched. She fought to keep it out of the ditch.

"Hold her steady, Nessa."

The other vehicle fell behind them again.

Landry pressed his back against her seat and thrust his arm out the window and took aim. The explosion of gun blasts startled her though she'd known they were coming.

Olivia heard Jeffrey's sharp intake of breath. Her attention rushed back and forth between the road ahead of her and the vehicle bearing down on her once more.

Another blast of gunfire. The passenger-side mirror flew apart. Jeffrey made a strained sound.

Landry returned fire.

Olivia's heart thundered but she ignored it. She had to drive. Had to get the hell out of the line of fire.

The rear window exploded. A bullet lodged in the dash, splitting the face cover of the digital clock.

Jeffrey yelped this time.

Enough.

"Buckle up, Landry."

She barely recognized her voice. Low, guttural.

"What?"

He twisted around and their eyes met in the rearview mirror. "Buckle up."

He didn't argue.

The instant she heard the click of his safety belt, she checked the vehicle behind her one last time. The vehicle was charging toward them again.

She waited, kept her speed steady.

Until he was almost on her bumper.

She stomped on her brake.

The vehicle rammed into the Explorer's rear bumper. The SUV fishtailed but she'd been ready for it. She cut the front wheels against the momentum of the rear, forcing the vehicle back under control without ever slowing her forward momentum.

The other car spun off into the ditch, the deployed air bags blinding the driver just long enough to ensure loss of control.

Olivia didn't realize she was smiling until she felt the muscles of her face straining with the effort.

"Stop this car!" Jeffrey, his eyes wide with terror,

had twisted around to stare at her. "Stop now, Olivia!"

She took a breath, only then noticing how her body was shaking. "I can't do that. You're going to have to stay calm and trust me."

He shook a finger in her direction, his expression dark with fear and anger. "No. I want you to stop this vehicle and tell me what the hell is going on. Those people may be injured back there! We should call someone…or…or do something!"

"They were trying to kill us." She kept her tone relatively calm, her voice low. She didn't need him going hysterical on her right now. Not that she could blame him. Any normal person would be hysterical after all that.

Landry sat forward, his reflection filling up the rearview mirror. "Settle down, Jeffery, and we might just survive this."

The fact that he braced his arms on the back of the front seat, his big ugly Glock in one hand, probably had more to do with Jeffrey's cooperation than anything Landry said.

"You're blocking my view." Olivia shot him a glower via the mirror he was currently dominating. She refused to note any of the details of his face. Not that she could see all that much with nothing more than the glow from the dash lights. But she didn't really need to see: she knew every line, angle and shadow by heart.

He scooted back from view. She was glad.

Olivia forced her attention back on the road. If she stayed on her present course, she could end up with another tail. She needed an alternate route. But first she needed answers.

Hamilton could have sent that tail, that much was true. But Landry could have been responsible for it just as easily. He could have set the whole thing up in an effort to regain her trust.

He might as well not waste his time. She trusted Hamilton far more than she did him.

Nothing Landry could do would change the way she felt about him. She hated him. Hated even the thought of him. Anger sizzled inside her but even that wasn't enough to completely block the hurt that she'd told herself repeatedly she'd put behind her. Evidently she hadn't put it as far behind her as she'd thought.

He'd ruined her life not once but twice.

He was toying with her now, keeping her guessing.

She took the next right. There was a small town an hour's drive from her current location. Once she'd gotten the SUV out of sight, she and Landry would face off.

His scent had already contaminated the air inside the vehicle. That tangy male scent she had never completely forgotten. She hated that it still affected her.

"I can drive if you'd like."

She closed her eyes a second to block her body's reaction to his voice. The vaguest hint of a British accent still lingered, no matter how hard he'd worked to conceal it. Nowhere man. He loved the idea that he could keep everyone guessing as to who he was and where he'd come from. Except when it was just the two of them...then he'd let his true self appear.

She'd heard that sexy voice in her dreams a thousand times. Had only just in the past year managed to go for months on end without dreaming about him.

Damn him for doing this.

Damn Hamilton for not seeing this coming.

"I guess that's a no."

She refused to rise to the bait. Chatting with him or having him look out for her in any way would be a betrayal to herself.

Her silence apparently got the message across. He didn't ask any more questions. Jeffrey didn't speak, either, but she had a feeling his reticence was related to shock.

Just when she'd started to relax, Landry's cooperation abruptly ended.

"I'm not sure you can trust Hamilton. He's the one who put the tail on us."

She told herself not to respond, not to give him the satisfaction of drawing her into a conversation, but she just couldn't hold back the blast of outrage.

"Don't waste your breath, Landry. I might not be able to trust Hamilton, but I definitely don't trust you."

"Ouch."

She gnashed her teeth nearly to the point of chipping the enamel.

"I guess I don't get credit for my past performance."

Heat roared up her neck and across her cheeks.

Images of them making love flooded her mind before she could derail that runaway train. That had been his intent. He'd wanted her to remember. Damn him.

She steeled herself against the feelings he hoped to resurrect. Reminded herself of all he'd taken from her.

Her right foot came down steadily on the brake. She whipped the SUV onto the side of the road. She wasn't waiting a second longer.

Whatever he wanted, she would know now.

Right here. Right now.

Even if it killed her.

Chapter 7

He was out of the backseat and standing toe to toe with her before any afterthought of caution could penetrate her mushrooming anger.

The Glock was still in his right hand, though the muzzle was aimed toward the ground. Her Beretta was held in a similar fashion. That he chose not to take a bead on her gave her little comfort. Holt Landry, the infamous Phantom, was an extremely dangerous man. No matter that his posture looked relaxed or that his expression appeared impassive, he could kill her at any time…if that was his intent. He was an expert in every manner of execution.

That he hadn't killed her already nudged at her curiosity.

She heard the front passenger-side door open. "Don't get out, Jeffrey," she ordered without taking her eyes off the enemy.

"Olivia, I'm calling the police."

Shit. She'd left her purse in the vehicle. "Just give me a minute, will you?" Even she heard the desperation in her voice. Dammit, she hated Landry for making her feel this way.

"For the record—" Jeffrey snapped—and he never snapped "—I think this whole thing has gone far enough!" Two tense beats of silence passed. "But if you're sure the two of you aren't going to kill each other, I can give you a minute, I suppose."

"Thank you."

Landry made a scoffing sound under his breath, igniting her fury all over again. He would make light of such a gesture of understanding and kindness; the man knew nothing about either.

"What do you want, Landry?" she demanded.

He inclined his head slightly. "To save your life. Is that such a bad thing?"

She steeled herself against her first reaction to his statement. Nothing he said could be trusted. Her entire existence had been compromised, including people she cared about. Somehow Landry was involved. She had to know how and why.

"All right." She stared straight into his eyes, looked past the mesmerizing blue color. Neither one of them had bothered to close their door, leaving the vehicle's interior light glowing just enough to provide a decent visual. It wouldn't actually matter if it was broad daylight—he would only show her what he wanted her to see anyway.

"Let's just assume for the moment that you are here to rescue me. Why do I need rescuing? I've been out of the business for three years. Who would be interested in anything related to who I am now?"

"Now there's where things get tricky. You see, because you're out of the business, I can't really share the details with you."

That old familiar lash of fury hurled her blood pressure into stroke zone. "Then I would suggest you start walking, old friend, because we're done."

Knowing full well that it could be the dead last thing she ever did, Olivia turned her back on him with the intent of climbing back into the Explorer and driving away.

"Wait."

She hesitated, told herself not to look back. But her need to know what the hell was going on won out.

"What?" She pivoted, sheltered somewhat in the cubicle created by the open doors.

Landry shoved the rear door shut and moved closer. So much for being sheltered. Her heart reacted as if three years ago hadn't happened. As if he weren't the enemy…as if she was the silliest damn fool on the planet.

"We have a lot to talk about, Nessa."

"I told you not to call me that." The sharpness of

her tone made him flinch. She blinked, certain she must have imagined it. Holt Landry never flinched.

"Just give me twenty-four hours. That's all I'm asking." His left forearm rested against her door, leaving her no escape route other than through that tall, muscular frame of his.

She almost agreed to his demand, but her brain kicked back into gear just in time. "We have nothing to talk about, Landry. You betrayed me three years ago. Left me in the cold to face the consequences of *our* actions."

Olivia let those old memories resurface. It had been *their* mission. He'd walked away unscathed while she'd faced certain punishment, costing her not only her career but her life as she knew it. The wrath had rushed in on her like a category-five hurricane. But then, she'd been the one to pull the trigger. He'd been there in a mere advisory, backup capacity.

His jaw hardened with whatever answer he had for her accusation. She wondered why he didn't say what was on his mind. This was his chance. His only chance. In about thirty seconds she was out of here. He and whoever the hell he was working for could just go ruin someone else's life. She wasn't playing that game again. Her agenda had changed in the last few minutes. She didn't care who'd resurrected her past or what they wanted. Her goal was to keep Jeffrey safe and to disappear. Some part of her understood that her goal was in many respects impractical but she refused to think about that in the face of this ghost from her past.

Incredibly, he looked away.

Olivia almost laughed out loud but her insides were too twisted into knots to manage the effort. What was she supposed to make of this? Was she supposed to believe that Landry had somehow grown a conscience in the past three years? That he cared enough to *rescue* her?

Yeah, right.

Men like Landry didn't have a conscience. Didn't have a heart. He was nothing but a machine—find the target, eliminate the target, walk away. As easy as one, two, three. No hesitation, no looking back.

When his gaze landed on hers once more, that impassive mask had fallen neatly back into place. "You're right. I should have been there. But we don't have time to rehash what should have been right now. You have to trust me, at least for a little while longer."

Olivia rolled her eyes and wrestled back the urge to burst into hysterical laughter. When she'd gotten a firm grip on her composure once more, she challenged, "Do you really expect me to fall for that line of crap? Are you nuts?" She shook her head. "I'm out of here."

This time, when she would have gotten into the Explorer, he wrapped the fingers of one hand around her arm. It wasn't so much the pressure of his hold that held her back: it was her own body's mutinous reaction that rendered her immobile. How could his mere touch devastate her so after all this time…after all she knew?

"Twenty-four hours, Vanessa. That's all I need. I can fix this, but you have to give me some time."

Odd, Hamilton had asked for the same thing. Twenty-four hours.

"Olivia, I don't know who this man is, but we shouldn't be sitting on the side of the road like this. Whoever sent those men could send someone else."

Her attention shifted to Jeffrey. She'd completely forgotten he was there. Christ. She had to be unstable. And he was right. They needed to keep moving. But first she had to make a decision about Landry.

"Jeffrey, I'll explain everything. I promise. Just give me a minute."

"I've been more than patient. I need some answers."

As if her life weren't complicated enough, Jeffrey did a total about face and went postal on her. He wrenched open his door and tried to get out with his seat belt still fastened. His outrage pumped even higher at the nuisance as he stabbed at the release button and slung off the belt. He jumped out of the Explorer and stormed around to where she and Landry stood. His nostrils actually flared. If she hadn't been so shocked she would have been impressed.

"Jeffrey," she reiterated, "I'll explain everything later."

He shook his head adamantly. "Later is now. I have the right to know what's going on here, Olivia. And why does he keep calling you Vanessa?"

That he looked ready to duke it out with Landry had her mouth gaping.

"Did you see the rear of this vehicle?" Jeffrey pointed in that direction, almost whopping Landry across the face in the process. "I hope you took the additional insurance coverage because I can tell you that the rental agency isn't going to be happy."

Shock? Mental breakdown? Olivia couldn't be sure. But this was not like Jeffrey. And it was definitely wasting valuable time.

"We've driven across the country. Broken into a man's home. Been chased by...by thugs and invaded by—" he glared at Landry "—by some sort of madman. What's next, Olivia?" His gaze swung back to her. "Are we going to knock off a bank?"

"Jeffrey—"

"Listen, my friend, we all need to calm down."

Jeffrey's as well as Olivia's gaze swerved toward Landry.

"Shut up, Landry. This has nothing to do with you." He had no right to speak to Jeffrey in that tone.

"You heard the lady," Jeffrey echoed as he bracketed his hands on his hips and thrust out his chin. "Shut up!"

Surprise vaulted through her. This was not the Jeffrey she knew. He looked like hell. His hair and clothes were tousled. He needed a shave. Clearly he was worried and overwrought. Had to be the pressure. Jeffrey Scott was not the demanding type and he certainly wasn't the sort to pick a fight...or to finish one, no matter the circumstances.

"Do you really expect me to take this from this

guy?" Landry asked, amusement simmering in his expression.

Bad had just gone to worse.

Before she could find her voice, Jeffrey amped up his glower at Landry. "Who do you think you are?"

Landry heaved a big breath and shoved his weapon into his waistband. "Sorry about this."

Had Olivia not been so startled by Jeffrey's actions, she might have seen Landry's next move coming.

But she didn't…not until it was too late.

Landry slugged Jeffrey.

Jeffrey crumpled like a leftover snowman in an East Coast spring thaw.

Olivia dropped to her knees next to his still body. "I swear, Landry." She aimed a death ray at him. "If you've hurt him I'll kill you."

Dammit. She smoothed the hair off Jeffrey's forehead. He was out cold. Fury charged through her. She muttered a few choice adjectives that described Landry perfectly, including traitor, asshole and a few others.

"He'll live."

Before she could argue, Landry scooped Jeffrey up and settled him into the backseat as if he weighed nothing.

"He'll need a seat belt," she snapped. Jeffrey never failed to wear his seat belt.

Landry looked annoyed but he did as she said. He tugged the middle safety belt around Jeffrey's waist and buckled it behind him. It wasn't exactly the way the design engineers intended, but it would help. It was anyone's guess what would happen next.

When Landry shut the door, he studied her a few moments, confusion lining his brow.

"What?" She wanted so bad to slug him on Jeffrey's behalf that it was all she could do not to act on the throbbing impulse.

"Where did you find this guy?" Landry shook his head. "He's not exactly your type, Nessa."

Enough. She'd had it with him. "You don't know a damn thing about me anymore, Landry. So just back off!"

He held up both hands in surrender. "Got it. We're wasting time here. The bottom line is your vehicle has been made. We need new wheels. Let's go back and get my SUV and we'll get the hell out of here. We need some distance and some time to sort this out."

Her free hand settled on her hip while her fingers tightened around the butt of the Beretta. "I didn't agree to give you the twenty-four hours, Landry. I'll take you back to your vehicle and then this little reunion is over."

Determination replaced his usually impassive expression. "You're going to get yourself and your friend killed."

Her gaze narrowed. How the hell could he expect her to trust him? What was he doing here? Why would he come barging back into her life?

"He's not my friend, Landry, he's my lover."

He made a rude sound. "Now I'm really impressed."

That urge to hurt him physically almost overwhelmed her a second time. "What's the location of your vehicle?"

"You drive," he countered. "I'll give you the directions."

It wouldn't have mattered if she'd said no or argued the point further. He walked around to the other side of the Explorer and got into the front passenger seat without waiting for her agreement or caring what she thought.

She got in, plopped her Beretta onto the console, slammed the door and shoved the gearshift into Drive. They'd spent all that time on the side of the road arguing and she still didn't know squat.

Olivia felt just as helpless as she had all those years ago when she'd fallen in love with him.

Why couldn't she learn from her mistakes?

Landry had parked his SUV down a side road not three miles from Hamilton's property. She didn't like returning to the scene of her last close encounter with trouble, but she had little choice.

Jeffrey had roused and maintained a vigil of silent fury.

Olivia would have a lot of explaining to do. Whatever she and Jeffrey had managed to build in the way of a relationship probably wouldn't survive this. Her whole life was shot to hell.

Again.

"You can get out now." She'd waited at least a minute for Landry to be on his way, but he just kept sitting there. "I told you I'd bring you back to your vehicle. I'd like to get on the road. I have a lot of highway to cover." She let her resolve speak for itself with the look she turned in his direction.

He swiveled in the seat to make eye contact. Dawn was creeping across the horizon, but here in the woods it was still damn dark. She could vaguely make out the seriousness in his expression with the negligible glow from the dash lights.

"This isn't one of those situations where there are options, Va..." He cleared his throat. "Olivia. There's only one way out of this situation and that's for us to work together. If we don't find out who started this, we can't stop him. If we don't stop him we'll end up dead. You know as well as I do that they won't stop until the job is done."

"Don't listen to anything he says, Olivia," Jeffrey interjected. "We should go directly to the nearest police station and turn him in."

Olivia offered Jeffrey a sympathetic look. She wanted to explain that it wasn't that easy but now wasn't a good time. Before she could attempt a reasonable response, Landry started talking again.

"The players have changed," he said, drawing her attention back to him. "Old enemies are now allies."

"I watch the news." He was going to have to give her something way bigger than that. "The whole world has changed. You think I live in a cave?"

"You don't understand. I'm not talking about what you see on the news. I'm talking about what goes on behind the scenes. The part you used to be involved in. That has changed. The things we know are now a liability."

She worked hard at not letting his words affect her, but she wasn't entirely successful. "What's that supposed to mean?"

"It means that we have something they want."

Olivia was tired. Tired and frustrated. "I don't have anything, Landry. I died, remember? I walked away with nothing but the clothes on my back and my life."

"What do you mean, you died?"

She sent another plea for patience in Jeffrey's direction.

"Don't say it," he grumped, "you'll explain everything later."

"We need to move," Landry pressed, drawing her attention back to him. "You know the routine. Hang around too long in one place and you'll get nailed to the wall."

"I'm not going anywhere with you, Landry." She'd trusted him once and, as he so eloquently put it, she'd gotten nailed to the wall. It wasn't going to happen again.

Those anonymous calls she'd gotten in the middle of the night abruptly joined the rest of the confusing thoughts swirling in her head.

"You've been watching me." The words came out a little too limply to pass as a true accusation, but she didn't need his confirmation. She knew it was him. On some level she'd always known.

"Yes." For the second time tonight he looked away, evidently fearing she would see something he didn't want her to see.

"Why?"

That deep blue gaze collided with hers. "Do you have to ask?"

A fire lit in her belly and she hated herself for the weakness he could so easily evoke deep inside her. This conversation had moved into treacherous territory. Treacherous in more ways than one.

"Get out, Landry." There was nothing soft or uncertain about her tone now. She wanted him gone.

He shook his head slowly. "I'm not going anywhere without you."

Talk about melodramatic.

Laughter bubbled up into her throat. This time she couldn't stop it from rushing out. "You're a head case. I have patients who are more grounded in reality than you. Now, get out. I'm not going anywhere with you. Stop wasting my time."

Again, her instincts failed her.

She should have seen his move coming, but she didn't.

The Beretta on her console was suddenly in his left hand, leaving her unarmed except for the knife in her boot and going for it would have been awkward to say the least.

She was, without doubt, a true idiot.

The Glock in his right wasn't aimed at her but that part was understood.

"Get your bags if you need them and get into the Land Rover."

"For the love of God!" Jeffrey leaned forward. "Are we being kidnapped now?"

"I suppose we have to do what the man says, Jeffrey." Her gaze met his and she hoped he understood that she had a plan. When he didn't argue she relaxed marginally. Though she doubted he liked her very much right now, she was certain Jeffrey considered her the lesser of the two evils currently plaguing his life.

Back to square one. Waiting for an opportunity.

She opened the door and slid out, snagging her handbag as she went. With a sharp thwack of her palm against his door as she passed, she ordered, "Let's get this over with, Jeffrey." Her hand stung but she needed the clarifying arc of discomfort.

Jeffrey got out behind her. Their gazes met again and she wanted to apologize for getting him into this, but nothing she could say would make any difference.

Besides, actions spoke louder than words. She intended to act. Now. She opened the cargo hatch and hefted her overnight bag onto her shoulder. The remainder of the money was inside. She would need it.

Jeffrey moved up next to her and grabbed his own bag.

Landry had already started toward the Land

Rover. Keeping one eye on him, she whispered, "Jeffrey."

He started at the sound of her voice, or maybe it was the fact that she whispered after all the yelling. "Yes?"

She jerked her head, indicating he should come closer as she slowly closed the Explorer's cargo door. "Where's the .32 I gave you?"

He frowned. "The gun?"

She shushed him and glanced covertly toward where Landry waited only a half-dozen yards away. "Where'd you put it?"

He patted his pants pockets. "I…" His hands came up, palms revealed and unfortunately empty. "I don't know. I must have lost it."

How could anyone lose a gun in the middle of a situation like this? Stay calm. This was Jeffrey. He wasn't familiar with the ins and outs of kill or be killed. The only thing he'd ever killed was a virus in a controlled lab environment. She couldn't take out her frustration on him.

"It's okay. We'll be fine." She said the last as much for herself as for his benefit.

Taking that morose walk in the direction of the Land Rover, Jeffrey rubbed his jaw as if he'd only just then remembered the sock he'd taken. "I'm going to press charges against him when this is over. I hope he has a good attorney." He looked down his shoulder at Olivia. "Even if he is a friend of yours." Realization dawned in his expression. "He's not one of your patients, is he?"

She supposed in Jeffrey's mind that would explain everything. What he would consider bizarre actions and strange stories could be expected from a mental case. "No. He's not."

Jeffrey looked disappointed.

Landry opened the rear hatch of his classic SUV and closed it again after they'd stowed their bags.

When he would have headed to the driver's door, he said to Olivia, "I'm sure you'll understand that I want you up front where I can keep an eye on you."

Nothing she hadn't expected.

He had worked with her before.

If they were enemies, which plainly was the case, he would be well aware that she would kill him in order to escape if necessary and, of course, given the opportunity. She understood that he would likely do the same.

Survival was the name of this game.

She'd played it too many times before.

Jeffrey, poor guy, didn't have a clue.

"Where is it we're going now, Landry?" Jeffrey settled into the backseat, clicked his seat belt into place and waited for an answer. "I'm as much a part of this as either of you. I have the right to know."

Jeffrey's determination not to be outdone by Landry continued to surprise her. But even that couldn't diminish her mounting frustration. She plopped into the front passenger seat and buckled up. Landry hadn't won, she reminded herself, he'd only bought himself some time. She wasn't done yet by any means. She still had the knife but he had at least two handguns. The right moment was crucial if she hoped to come out of a confrontation alive.

Landry started the engine. "To a safe location," he told Jeffrey as he shifted into Reverse and executed a three-point turn that set the vehicle in the direction of the main highway.

"Are we supposed to trust you and not ask any questions?" Jeffrey inquired further, his tone crisp.

"Trust might be too much to ask," Landry admitted. "For now, I'll settle for cooperation."

Olivia wanted to punch him for sounding so cool and collected. He was in charge and that was the way he liked it. She thought of the knife in her boot. Oh, she'd cooperate, all right. She'd be a real team player, all the way up to the moment that she sank that blade right into his black heart. Her chest tightened.

She closed her eyes and fought the confusing and contradictory emotions. Over and over she told herself how much she wanted to hurt him. But those feelings were nothing more than a self-defense mechanism. All the psychology in the world wouldn't whitewash that glaring fact. She couldn't kill him or even hurt him unless it was in self-defense or to protect Jeffrey. Still, it made her feel better to think about it.

How could he possibly still have any sort of control over her? She'd hated him too long.

But what if he was telling her the truth? What if

he had gotten a tip and had come to head off her elimination? She gave her head a little shake. It was way too early in the game for her to even guess. Right now, no one was exempt from suspicion.

"I suppose I can cooperate," Jeffrey announced, sounding rather cool and collected himself. "As long as Olivia is agreeable."

She hoped like hell his sticking by her didn't cost him far more than he'd bargained for.

Chapter 8

They didn't go that far.

Less than an hour from Hamilton's weekend getaway. They hadn't even left the state of Virginia. But the back roads he'd taken weren't familiar. Maybe fifty miles south of Arlington, not that much farther from D.C. proper. The last fifteen or so miles she couldn't say for sure which way they'd been traveling.

A long driveway that led onto a wooded property ended in a clearing where an ancient farmhouse stood, its metal roof glistening in the rising sun.

The place looked old. Not run-down, just old. Like something straight out of the 1800s. A porch in front and half a dozen paned windows waited in the shadows. No indication of occupancy. No vehicles. Not even a dog.

"Gee, and I was hoping for a heavenly bed and a hot tub."

Landry shut off the engine. "It isn't as rustic as it looks."

Olivia knew without asking that this place did not belong to Landry. It wasn't his style. She assumed the house belonged to a friend, though, unless he'd changed drastically, she doubted he had many friends.

No one liked perfection. Landry was physically gorgeous, mentally sharp and unerring in his work.

Stop it. Don't go there.

She would not start dwelling on the assets that had once drawn her to him.

"As long as it has indoor plumbing," she noted, opening her door, "I'll be happy for about two minutes."

Jeffrey emerged from the backseat and made a harrumphing sound as he took in their quarters.

Landry opened the cargo door and grabbed Olivia's bag before she could.

"I can handle it, Landry." His move wouldn't be about chivalry. It would have everything to do with making sure she had no means of opportunity at her disposal, including whatever she'd packed. He would anticipate backup supplies. They'd had similar training.

"I've got it."

He strode toward the house without bothering to ensure she followed.

Olivia surveyed the property. It wasn't like she was going anywhere. They were miles from civilization and the only means of transportation belonged to the man from whom she needed to escape.

Question was, could she manage it?

Jeffrey grabbed his bag and closed the hatch. He studied Olivia a long moment. "Are you okay? I'm not sure what's really going on here, but I'm very concerned about you. This man—" he glanced toward the house "—doesn't appear to actually want to hurt you. At least I assume if he'd wanted us dead, we would be dead by now. But I'm getting mixed signals from him."

Very astute, she mused. Jeffrey's continued concern for her was like a kick in the stomach. She hugged him. Couldn't help herself. "I'm fine, Jeffrey." She let go a weary breath. "I'll get us out of this, I swear."

"And I'll help," he promised with a faint smile. "Whatever threatens you, threatens me."

She hadn't deserved this man. He was too good. Too kind. She'd only been kidding herself with the idea that her life could ever be normal.

When she stepped back from the embrace and turned to the house that would either be their refuge or their prison, her gaze met Landry's. He stood on the porch, watching. His thoughts on what he'd just witnessed were carefully schooled behind that impassive mask he always wore.

Without missing a beat, Olivia strode straight up

to the porch, climbed the steps and looked him square in the eye. "I hope you've got food in there."

Landry nodded once. "We'll eat, then we'll talk."

Talk. So he could tell her a few more lies?

Talk wasn't on her mind. Finding that opportunity she needed for escape was her one goal.

She pinned a wide smile into place. "While you cook, we'll freshen up."

Something changed in Landry's expression but she couldn't quite decipher the transition. Maybe he didn't like the idea of the two of them getting out of his sight together.

Tough.

"Come on, Jeffrey." She walked inside without waiting for an official invitation or a guided tour. The house wasn't that large. She could find her own way around.

"Leave your cell phones with me," Landry ordered, halting her march across the living room.

She tossed her handbag onto the antiquated plaid sofa. Jeffrey's phone was in her bag, as well. With a quick survey of the room she summed up the decorating theme as out-of-date country with a lean toward comfortably worn.

With an acerbic look in Landry's direction when he remained silent, she asked, "What about my bag?"

"It's all yours." He gave her a look that said he'd checked it out and wasn't worried about the contents.

How very gracious of him. She snatched her bag off the knotty pine table at the end of the sofa.

He indicated the hall to the right of the kitchen that lay straight ahead. "Make yourselves at home."

Passing the wide entry to the kitchen, she made a mental note that there was a back door just past the stove. Along the hall to the right of the kitchen was a bath with one small window, and beyond were three bedrooms. She chose door number two on the right side of the hall, the bedroom that faced the front and side of the property. She dumped her bag onto the bed. Jeffrey deposited his next to hers.

He sniffed. "My allergies are not going to like this place."

Poor Jeffrey. He'd been so patient. And so heroic. She patted his arm. "Don't worry. We won't be here long."

He looked relieved. "You have a plan?"

"Yes." She eased to the door and checked the hall. She heard shuffling of metal and stoneware in the kitchen. Landry was occupied for the moment. But that didn't mean he couldn't hear. He could have listening devices hidden all over this house for all she knew.

She turned back to Jeffrey. "We need a shower."

Again he appeared taken aback. "Is it safe? I mean, is it wise to turn our backs on him long enough to shower?" He shook his head. "I don't trust the man. He's taking this hostage thing too far. Are you sure he's not from one of the psych wards where you've volunteered? I hear there are some real crazies in those state-run institutions."

Patience. Thinning at its current rate, she wasn't sure how much longer she'd be able to hang on to that precious commodity. Jeffrey was the last person she should be short with.

"He's not one of my patients. There are things I have to tell you. But right now we don't have time. You have to trust me."

He lifted one skeptical eyebrow. "That's what he said."

She offered him a reassuring face. "But you know me, Jeffrey."

More skepticism. "Do I?"

Okay, so maybe that wasn't the right way to go. "We don't have time to go into that right now. Let's freshen up."

She grabbed a change of clothes from her bag. Jeffrey, still looking dubious, did the same. They headed to the only bathroom in the house. Olivia closed and locked the door more to annoy Landry than to ensure they weren't disturbed. If Landry wanted in, he could definitely get in. A mere slab of wood would never stop him.

The tub was ancient but clean and, thankfully, a showerhead had been added in recent years, along with the necessary curtain. She turned on the water and quickly stripped off her travel-weary clothes. Jeffrey moved a little slower, but with her encouragement he was undressed in no time and she tugged him into the shower.

He pulled her into his arms before she could stop

him and she was the one surprised when his arousal nudged her intimately.

"It's good to hold you like this, Olivia."

For a couple of seconds she let herself enjoy the familiar comfort of his well-toned body and the idea that some things hadn't changed. Jeffrey might not be a player like Landry, but he stayed fit and was quite handsome. He was kind and polite…and safe. She'd found the latter soothing. She had enjoyed their relationship. She would miss him…they would never be able to go back to the way things were.

Right now, however, she had to focus. Flattening her palms against his chest to restrain his growing interest in turning this shower into a quickie, she explained, "Maybe later. Right now we need to talk about what's going on and what we're going to do about it."

His embrace loosened a little but not entirely. "All right. I suppose all the excitement served as an aphrodisiac. What would you like me to do?"

Keeping her voice low enough that the sound of the water provided sufficient camouflage, she laid out her plan, such as it was.

"Since he has control of the weapons, I'm going to have to rely upon hand-to-hand combat."

Jeffrey's expression turned somber. "That's too dangerous. Let me have a shot at him."

She pressed her fingers to his lips. "Keep your voice down."

"Sorry." He cleared his throat. "He could kill both

of us. We can't be sure of his intentions. I can sense that you don't entirely trust him. Why take the risk?"

"Because there's no other choice. We can't sit idly by while he does whatever he has planned. I have to make a move. This isn't going to be over until I figure out what the hell is going on. I can't do that here."

He pursed his lips and thought about what she'd said for long enough to make her nervous. Any attempt she made at escape would be doomed if she couldn't count on Jeffrey.

"I'm not sure I understand any of this. You said one of your patients had threatened me to get back at you, for some perceived injustice, I presume. You said the man you visited last night was a relative of this patient. I'm clear up to that point. How does this Landry fellow play into things if he's not your patient?"

More lies. "I'm not even sure about that myself." How much should she tell him at this point? Not much. "We were friends once." She hated that the old pain and disillusionment slipped into her tone so easily. "But he betrayed me and for some reason he's back now. I don't know his reasons, but I need to find out. Somehow it's all connected." That was about as clear as mud.

"You were more than friends."

At Jeffrey's suggestion, her gaze met his. The guardedness she saw there sent another stab of regret deep into her chest. There was no reason to lie about that. He was too smart not to pick up on the signs. If she looked at the situation from Jeffrey's perspective, this thing between her and Landry was the only tangible part.

"Yes," she confessed, "we were more than friends."

He nodded sagely. "That explains the way he looks at you."

She felt his arms tighten possessively around her. "We were over a long time ago, Jeffrey." It wasn't that her relationship with Jeffrey, or what was left of it, was such that she needed to explain that aspect of her past. But she wanted to…for some reason. It simply felt like the right thing to do under the circumstances.

Jeffrey didn't respond to her assertion. Attempting to convince him would be a waste of time. He either believed her or he didn't. They had plans to make and the water was cooling already.

She grabbed the bar of soap and began to lather her body as she explained more of her plan. "I'll take whatever opportunity arises to regain control. And when I do, I need you to be ready to move."

He took the bar she offered and lathered his skin. "I'll follow your lead," he assured. "Anything to get us out of this situation."

That was all she needed. "Just stay alert and be ready."

"I will. I won't breathe easy again until we're back in L.A."

She didn't tell him that going back to L.A. right now would be too dangerous. He wouldn't take it well. She let him believe that they were on the same sheet of music. That was the best for the moment.

Thankfully, a bottle of store-brand shampoo prevented the need to use bar soap on her hair. When they'd finished their shower and dried sufficiently, getting dressed was accomplished much more quickly. Olivia's hair would just have to dry on its own since she didn't find a dryer.

Besides, if Jeffrey was half as starved as she was, the scent of bacon frying was driving him mad. It definitely put some additional enthusiasm into her desire to rejoin Landry.

Olivia was glad she'd packed for comfort. Jeans, T-shirt and the hiking boots. The knife was sheathed and tucked in the right one.

The scent of bacon and toast had permeated the air in the hall and the living room beyond it. Olivia's stomach rumbled as she entered the kitchen and got a visual on the source of the pleasant smells. Toast, bacon, eggs, O.J. and coffee. She couldn't believe Landry had gone to all this trouble.

Jeffrey pulled a chair from the table for her and took the one right next to it for himself. Landry plunked a plate in front of each of them before placing a third on the opposite side of the table. He poured the juice and coffee before claiming his chair. She gritted her teeth and tried her best not to focus on those capable hands or those broad shoulders. Domestic duty only made him appear sexier. How was that possible?

Olivia directed her thoughts back to business and reached for the coffee first. "I see you haven't lost your touch in the kitchen."

Landry grunted something that couldn't quite be called an affirmative response, but she took it as one all the same. He had always been very handy in the kitchen. Whenever they were together, if they dined in, he did the cooking. He'd claimed that, being raised by his mother without the influence of a father, he'd had no choice but to learn to prepare an appetizing meal or expire from sheer boredom. There'd been no one to teach him outdoor activities.

Olivia was pretty sure the cooking was more a hobby that provided an extreme counterpoint to what he did for a living. Being an Interpol agent was very much like working for the CIA. Depending upon your division, the work could be murder—literally. All agents needed ways to relieve stress. The other way they'd relieved their stress bobbed to the surface of her musings. She shifted in her chair, ordering herself to stop thinking about him in that way.

Like Olivia's had been until three years ago, Landry's position was assassin. Quickly, surgically, without any fuss or fanfare. Do the job, get out, end of story.

So when he was at home he created meals like a master chef and lived the quiet life of a well-heeled man of means. She'd been to his Notting Hill home in London. Landry had money. She had always felt that his quiet, reserved life in England had prompted him into the business of master spy and assassin out of sheer boredom. He was very good at what he did. Which explained nothing about why he was here, serving her eggs and bacon, a typical American breakfast.

But he'd said they would talk after they'd eaten.

Fair enough.

Landry glanced across the table at Jeffrey. "I hope you like scrambled. It seemed the safest route."

"Scrambled is fine." Jeffrey placed his paper napkin on his lap and dug into his meal with the same precision and care with which he did everything else. Including his lovemaking.

Olivia told herself to eat. She would need the energy and she was famished, but her attention kept drifting across the damn table to their insistent host. No matter how she tried to keep her thoughts on other things.

He hadn't changed that much in the past three years. Not that she wanted to notice. Last night, between the surprise of seeing him, the insanity of the circumstances and the darkness, she hadn't really looked at him all that much. Or maybe she'd realized how dangerous it would be to do so.

Somehow, in the light of day or perhaps in her sleep-deprived state, she couldn't suppress the urge, nor could she slow her own body's foolish reaction.

His hair was raven black. He still wore it short. The blue eyes even now managed to prompt that same old effect on her, sending her pulse into overdrive. She yearned to look too long, which would only lead to getting lost in the memories of how good it had been between them. That lean, chiseled face didn't help, either. Nor did the fact that his well-formed jaw was dressed in a day's beard growth. Top that off with lips fuller than the typical male's and you had big trouble. The fluttering in her chest punctuated the thought.

And that was only the beginning. Then there were those broad shoulders and a tall, muscular frame that got a second look wherever he went. A cocky stride and just enough of a British accent, when he chose to use it, to have the women fawning over every word. Olivia was pretty sure he did that part on purpose. He could speak with a Southern brogue when he wished. He'd admitted to her once that he'd lived in so many places and taken on so many identities that he wasn't sure if he even had an accent anymore without consciously adding one.

There you have it. Good-looking, charming, intelligent—and deadly.

That was Holt Landry.

Furious at herself for getting caught up in those incredible outer trappings, she forced her full attention to her plate. Think about something safe. In sharp contrast to her past choices, she'd chosen Jeffrey in her new life. He was attractive in a bookish sort of way. His hair was a sandy brown, his eyes a deep, rich cocoa. His face was handsome in a classic, nonspectacular way. He had an athletic body but it was too lean to be called muscular. He had no accent really, just a very polite, professional way of speaking. He was charming, extremely intelligent and completely safe and reliable.

Here they all three sat. Thrown together by circumstances she had yet to comprehend.

She needed feedback from Hamilton but wasn't sure contacting him again would be in her best interest.

She needed Landry to come clean with her.

She couldn't fully trust either of them. No matter how much she wanted to depend on Hamilton, she couldn't be absolutely sure. She knew this game too well.

Bottom line, she was on her own.

When Jeffrey's fork was nestled next to an empty plate, Olivia decided it was time. She'd picked at her food, but she was good to go.

"Jeffrey, do you mind giving us some privacy? Landry and I need to talk." She met Jeffrey's gaze, hoping he'd remember their talk in the shower. "Didn't I see that book you've been reading in your overnight bag?"

A frown tugged his eyebrows together. "I don't…" Her meaning hit him. "Yes. Sure, I'll read." He pushed back from the table and stood. "Thanks, Landry. I can't say that I appreciate your high-handed tactics but the meal was decent."

Jeffrey took his dishes to the sink and then left the room. She wasn't afraid to allow him out of her sight. He wouldn't dare leave her on her own with

Landry. Jeffrey was far too reliable to let her down like that.

When the sound of the bedroom door closing behind him reached her ears, Olivia said to Landry, "I hope you're ready to come clean now."

"Speaking of cleaning." He stood. "You wash and I'll dry."

She got up, wanted to hit him for yet another attempt at putting her off. "As long as you can talk at the same time."

His gaze claimed hers in a knowing look that caused the air in her lungs to evaporate. "I think you know I can."

The fire in his eyes so startled her with its intensity that it set off little explosions of heat deep in her loins. "Let's get to it then." Her verbal response set off more of those fiery flares in his blue eyes.

At least they were even. She wasn't the only one affected by memories of the past.

Since there was no dishwasher, doing the dishes the old-fashioned way was the only option. She filled the sink, then plunged her hands into the hot, sudsy water and began with the glasses and cups.

"Al Hadi was a righteous hit."

She almost dropped the glass in her hand. That he would say that to her, after disappearing three years ago and leaving her with no one to back up her story, detonated years of pent-up fury.

"How dare you say that to me after you walked

away like it never happened?" Her gaze zeroed in on his and instead of seeing that mesmerizing color, all she saw was the object of the hatred she'd been nurturing for so long.

"I had no choice, Nessa."

Her fingers tightened so around the glass she had to consciously let it drop back into the water to prevent crushing it.

"You knew everything," she accused. "You were privy to the orders. You were my backup, damn you." She braced herself against the counter, frothy water dripping from her wet hands. All the pain and disappointment from that time came flooding back. "You could have stood up for me. Told the truth. But you didn't. You left me with no proof of my story."

The orders had been "eyes only," clad in the highest level of security utilized. Her mission was simple. Take out the man poised to assume power over a small, little-known Middle Eastern country much like Kuwait. Oil rich and an important fledgling ally to the American government. But the new leader rising to power would change that pivotal fact. The long-term analysis of his rise to power was that he would negatively influence other countries in the region.

She'd had her orders, she had carried them out. Al Hadi was dead inside of seventy-two hours once she'd arrived in-country. Not once in her entire career had she ever failed on a mission.

She'd wished a thousand times since that she had failed that once.

"Interpol wouldn't let me get involved." He leaned one hip against the counter next to her, pressing her with his proximity. "I wanted to, but they ordered me to stand down and just to be sure I did, they put me under house arrest. I had no choice in the matter."

"How terrible for you." She snarled the words. Wanted to bang her fists against his chest until she shattered his cold heart the way he'd shattered hers.

"And then they told me you were dead."

She told herself not to believe the pain she read in his face as well as his tone. No way would she let him sway her. He hadn't cared what happened to her. He'd proven that beyond a shadow of a doubt when he disappeared, leaving her to fight for her life.

"Hamilton is the only reason I'm still alive," she reminded him. "It damn sure wasn't because of anything *you* did."

He nodded. "I can't deny that. It was months before I figured out the truth—that you were still alive. That I'd been used and lied to."

Memory of that first year, the pain and the regret that had been almost unbearable, manacled her in its agonizing grip. No one had been there for her. She'd been completely and devastatingly alone. "And you did nothing to try and find me," she guessed. "Until you had your own selfish agenda."

He moved his head from side to side, the motion barely a move at all. "I found you four months after my superior informed me of your death."

Emotion burned at the backs of her eyes, but she'd be damned if she'd let him see it. The hurt and anger pounded against her chest like a tidal wave. "You son of a bitch, you *knew?*"

Landry clamped strong hands around her wrists and held her still when she would have walked away, forcing her to look at him. "At first I stayed away because I was afraid my coming near you would put you in danger." He hesitated before going on. "Then...you seemed happy, so I stayed away to make sure you continued to be happy. But when I got wind something related to your status was going down, I had to step in."

"You got wind of what?" she demanded. How could she trust anything he told her? No matter how badly some ridiculously vulnerable part of her wanted to...she couldn't put herself in that position again. Every instinct told her that he was holding out on her...that he knew more than he was telling.

"Someone was going to use you again. I couldn't let that happen. What they did to you three years ago was wrong."

She wrenched loose from his hold. What *they* did to her. Funny how he left himself out of the scenario. "I've played those days over and over in my head. I don't know who set me up back then, I have no clue who it is now. How could you possibly hope to figure it out?" Nothing he said would make a difference, because there was no way she would believe him. This whole conversation was a monumental waste of time and emotion.

"I was chosen for that assignment three years ago for a reason, Olivia. You know how it works. When your country has a high-level, high-risk international operation like that, mine plays the watchdog and vice versa. It was my job to make sure no one crossed certain lines. I was set up the same as you were."

There was some truth to what he said. Whenever the CIA and Interpol worked together on an operation of that sensitive a nature, one side did the dirty work while the other served as a sort of referee, ensuring no unnecessary boundaries were breached.

"But you walked away unscathed," she threw back at him. "You didn't lose everything the way I did."

"You're right," he relented. "I did walk away unscathed. But it wasn't because I wanted to. The question now is, why is someone digging up the ugly past?"

She moved her head slowly from side to side. "I don't know. I can only assume they feel threatened somehow by my existence."

"There was a rumor," he began, looking thoughtful, "that the real reason the CIA dropped their support was because Al Hadi refused to bend to their demands. They'd had a deal and he bowed out rather ungracefully, thus turning the tide on how the CIA viewed him."

He couldn't know that for sure any more than she did. "What demands? Al Hadi was the one working against the U.S. If he'd assumed power, the U.S.

might have lost all credibility in the region. You know that." The CIA didn't go onto foreign soil and wreak havoc unless it served the greater good. "He had to have done something far more detrimental than simply walking away from negotiations." That was the only information she'd been given; it was all she'd needed. She'd had her orders.

"The way I heard it, the CIA had made certain promises to Al Hadi," Landry suggested. "In return for carrying out those promises, he would provide an abundant source of oil as well as unification influence—everything the U.S. needed in that region. Imagine the economic and political benefits."

Yeah, she mused, the price of gasoline wouldn't be sky-high. She grabbed the dish towel and dried her damp hands. They could theorize all they wanted, but they would never know what really happened. "So what? That doesn't prove what happened then and it sure as hell doesn't explain what's happening now. Face it, the truth is beyond our grasp, Landry. We can't hope to know for sure. You, of all people, should understand that."

"I understand that choosing to assassinate a political leader simply because he changed his mind on a topic and wouldn't play nice is dirty business no matter how you look at it," he confessed. "Very un-PC. That's why the CIA covered it up, calling it a bad op before the media could get a whiff of the stink. For future reference, the Agency had to have a fall guy—or woman, as the case turned out to be. It's called insurance. No one likes the past to come back and bite them in the ass."

She didn't want to keep going over and over this. "I can't change the past, Landry. I know what they did to me. Nothing I did then…nothing I do now is going to alter the facts. The only thing *I* can do is try to stop whoever hauled me back into this."

"Then your beef is with me."

More of that unexpected shock she'd been experiencing hurtled through her. She tossed the dish towel back on the counter. "Are you admitting that you started this whole mess?"

A firm shake of his head followed by, "I didn't start it, Vanessa, I derailed it. You had been targeted. I was informed. I knew the only way you'd pay attention was if I activated your code name and used your boyfriend as the bait. It was the only possible way I could hope to get your full attention."

She felt stunned. "I knew it was you. Who the hell was Soderbaum?"

"A retired agent who owed me a favor."

The fury that threatened to erupt inside her was hampered by so many other emotions that she wasn't sure which one to pick from. "You lured me into this trap." Her gaze held his, searched for any sign of deceit. "You risked Jeffrey's safety…ruined my life all over again—"

"I probably saved your life, Nessa."

She slugged him. Couldn't stop herself. Didn't even realize the synapse had occurred until her fist made contact with his jaw. This time he was the one who didn't see the move coming.

He didn't sway but he damn well flinched. Her breath sawed in and out of her lungs in an effort to keep up with her racing heart. How could he do this to her? Wasn't once enough?

"I guess I deserved that." He rubbed his jaw. "However angry you are with me right now, Nes...Olivia, remember that unless we determine the source of the threat to you, you could end up dead. I doubt your friend Jeffrey would be pleased if we let that happen."

"Wait," she snapped as she massaged her forehead, tried to block the ache that had started there. "Why would anyone want to dig this back up now? Is there some political agenda I don't see?" If anyone appreciated the idea of not having the past come back to haunt them, she did, but she didn't see what this particular past had to do with the present. "Who's your source, Landry? Who told you I had been targeted for elimination?"

"That's a little complicated." He turned back to the sink and gestured for her to resume her duty of washing.

She wanted to scream. But she knew him too well. He wouldn't continue until she did as he asked. Olivia stuck her hands into the water and grabbed another glass, careful not to take her frustration out on it.

"The political agenda is not yet clear to me," he admitted. "But whatever it is, you can rest assured that it ties in closely with what happened on that final mission. Otherwise you wouldn't be in line for elimination."

"I'm following you so far." She wouldn't say she agreed with his conclusions. She didn't have enough information to form a solid conclusion, and neither did he, it appeared. All she had was his word that a source he wouldn't reveal had tipped him off. Not exactly something she could or would take to the bank.

Landry took the glass she'd just washed and rinsed it. "When Al Hadi changed his mind about supporting the U.S., for whatever reason, the CIA had him eliminated, ensuring that the other candidate, Bahir, won the election."

What did that prove? "Bahir, as I recall, was far less influential in the region than Al Hadi." She shrugged, trying to see the value in his point. "Still, I suppose it ultimately worked out." From what she had seen in the news, things had turned out just the way the CIA had wanted. It had taken a little more time, but hey, that was life.

Landry slowly turned the towel around the glass he'd rinsed. "Bahir is a man easily controlled but one who lacks any scruples at all. He could turn any time. All he needs is the proper motivation. The details of your final mission could provide lots of motivation. I'm certain the CIA will do anything to make sure that never happens."

She passed the last of the glasses to him. That was

true of any politician. She didn't know a single one who could be trusted. Why even talk about this? "Do you have reason to believe the U.S. should be worried?" The way he persisted along these lines, surely he had his reasons.

"I do." He put the glass away. "I believe that tenuous balance is part of our current problem."

His theory wasn't totally off the mark. "I'll buy that, but it still doesn't explain what it has to do with me or my final assignment with the CIA." She handed him a freshly washed cup. "I was the one who took the fall. I was written up as a rogue agent, suspected of treason, et cetera. That's why Hamilton took me out of the picture. Faked my death. No one would come after a dead agent."

He dried the cup and stowed it as he had the glasses, then leveled his gaze on hers. "I can't give you the answers you're looking for just yet. I only know that someone wants you dead, and if they want you dead, that means they want *me* dead."

"Why you?" He'd walked away clean last time. Why would anyone drag him back into this?

"They—whoever *they* are—have to know that I was privy to the same details as you. Wouldn't that make me a target, as well?"

Possibly. Both she and Landry were low profile. They could be eliminated, blamed for the Agency's past mistakes, and no one would really care. The facts were that she'd assassinated the candidate poised to win the election three years ago. The sitting president, Umar, had been a staunch enemy of the U.S., but his health had deteriorated to the point that he could no longer intimidate the people into keeping him in power. What relevance did those facts have now? If she and Landry were targets for what they knew, why wouldn't Hamilton be one, as well?

Then again, maybe he was too high profile to easily eliminate.

She stared out the window over the sink, looking at nothing at all. There was simply no way to form a reasonable theory. "This is going to end badly, Landry." The realization came suddenly, with an intensity that shook her. Maybe the current political climate and the relations between the U.S. and some little Middle Eastern country that most people couldn't even locate on a map had nothing at all to do with her dilemma. Maybe the bottom line was that she hadn't been meant to survive that last mission. It could be as simple as that.

Now that mistake had to be rectified.

The urgency in Hamilton's voice when he'd told her three years ago that there was no other way to save her outside faking her death had broadsided Olivia. He'd wanted her out of the way as quickly as possible. Had pushed her to agree to his hasty plan.

She turned back to Landry once more. "Hamilton was in charge of the entire operation. He was the one who confirmed my orders. Now here I am, caught up in the game again. When no one else knew I was still alive but him. But why would he do this after he saved my life?"

She didn't want to believe that possibility. But it held far too much merit to ignore. Hell, it was the only feasible possibility she even had right now if she believed anything Landry had told her.

Landry lifted his shoulders and let them fall. "Maybe. But he isn't the only one who had access to this information. You must know that."

"Director Woods?" Hamilton was only the deputy director of field operations. Woods was his superior. Landry was right, she supposed. Woods would likely have known most every step Hamilton made. Or, at least, that was the way it was supposed to work.

Landry nodded an affirmative. "Along with a couple of others."

"But Hamilton was the only one who knew I was still alive," she argued. As much as she didn't want to believe it was him, he was the most likely suspect. Disillusionment turned the breakfast she'd eaten minutes ago into an unyielding rock in her stomach. He was the only one.

Except Landry. He'd already admitted that he'd somehow known she was alive almost from the beginning. And now he'd blown her cover. Olivia lost whatever cool she'd had left at that precise instant. She slugged him again, this time with everything she had. She didn't knock him off his feet but he definitely staggered a bit.

"A repeat performance wasn't necessary," he grumbled, rubbing his jaw again.

"The first time was for trying to get me killed."

Not to mention Jeffrey, she didn't say. "This time was just for being a jerk."

"Bloody hell, Vanessa, I'm not trying to get you killed. I'm trying to help you."

"In case you haven't noticed, I was doing fine without you or your help."

"But danger was headed your way," he urged, his voice soft and compelling. "I had to do something. I couldn't stand back and let them take your life away again. They took everything, Nessa. Stole who you were." He pressed a hand to his chest. "Stole who *we* were."

"And you want me to believe that all I lost somehow mattered to you." Like she would believe that in this lifetime.

His fingers curled around her upper arms and pulled her closer. She told herself to resist, but it didn't happen. "It matters," he murmured.

He couldn't possibly mean what it sounded like he meant.

"What are you saying?"

"Olivia? Are you all right?"

Her attention swung to the kitchen door. Jeffrey stood there looking suspect and immensely concerned.

She shrugged off Landry's touch. "I'm fine." She glanced at Landry. "We're finished here."

She walked out of the kitchen. She needed to think. Without the presence of her past, recent or otherwise.

Chapter 9

Olivia sat on the back porch, staring at the place where the grass gave way to the woods. She imagined that at one time the dense forest had owned this clearing. Sometime in the last hundred or so years the owner had made way for the house, changing the landscape forever.

That was what the CIA had done to her. They'd cut down her career—her life—and changed the landscape forever. She knew it wasn't fair to blame the Agency in general. This was the result of decisions made by one or two. People who liked playing God. Power-hungry bastards who cared only for themselves. She'd taken the fall for a mistake. The price was her life as she knew it.

She sucked a deep breath of fresh air into her lungs and expelled it slowly. Why hadn't he left it alone?

She'd gotten used to the fact that her preferred career was over. With no family ties, vanishing had been easy. Well, easy might be an overstatement, but certainly doable.

For months she'd grieved the loss of her career, of her former self. Of *him*.

Somehow, maybe because of her training in the workings of the mind, she'd managed to fall into sync with her new existence. She'd built a new career along with a very basic life. Had made a couple of friends. Her patients were eccentric but they paid the bills. There had been a long line of one-night stands and then she'd met Jeffrey. Her life had begun to feel…normal.

But she wasn't normal. She would never be normal.

She'd taken so many lives in the line of duty. The reality of that career had taken a toll once she'd been still long enough to dwell on it. Once she'd truly lived among the "normals" and had to face the differences between herself and others…civilians.

Maybe that was why she'd never committed fully to Jeffrey. Better the possibility that her former career had handicapped her in the area of emotions than the idea that she was still in love with Landry. Tamping down even the concept, she mentally moved on. There was no way to change the events that had occurred recently. Landry or Hamilton or maybe both had seen to that. If she intended to have a future, she had to have a plan.

Or maybe Landry had one. *Yeah, right.*

He had given her up. Oh, he had his excuses, just like last time. That made twice he'd screwed her in the most negative sense of the word. Yet his theory about why someone had targeted her for elimination contained so many elements of truth it would be hard to label any single part of it a lie.

Did she trust him or not?

She just didn't know. The first thing she needed to do was find out Landry's precise plans, if he had any. She knew him well enough to know he wouldn't start something he didn't have a scheme for finishing. That he might very well be using her for bait fired her up but the deed was done. Finding out the reason had to be her next move.

Uncertainty warred with her sense of reason when she considered he'd insinuated that she mattered. But she couldn't trust her emotions where he was concerned. Letting him get to her via the past would be a major mistake.

She'd just have to play it by ear and hope that all her better instincts would check in before she got in too deep.

The only problem was what to do with Jeffrey.

Dragging him along wouldn't be practical or safe. She couldn't let him go back to L.A. in the event whoever was after her attempted to force her location out of him. She now knew that he had never been a

target, but that didn't mean it was safe for him to resume his everyday life. Not until this was over.

Maybe taking him along was the only alternative.
At least that way she could make sure no one else
got to him. But there was no way to guarantee she
could protect him. It was a no-win situation.

Regret that her past had propelled him into this
mess sliced deep.

That was the thing, she supposed, that made the
difference in being able to live with her former profession on any level. Every single target she'd ever
neutralized had been a player. People who understood the risks, who willingly took those chances for
their own personal gain. Not necessarily bad guys,
but enemies nonetheless. That was the difference. No
one she'd eliminated had been an innocent. Not even
the final target, whose elimination had cost her everything. Though he evidently shouldn't have been
a target, he'd still been a player in the game of world
domination. His number had simply come up prema-
turely because of some asshole's personal agenda.

Jeffrey, however, was a true innocent. Being in
any way responsible for his death was not acceptable.

Damn Landry for putting her in this position.

Maybe if she told Jeffrey the truth, he would be
reasonable and listen to her on the issue of staying
out of sight until this was over. It was worth a shot.

Determined to get things started toward a resolu-
tion, she went inside in search of the men involved
in this disaster.

Jeffrey sat on the couch looking sorely out of place, with the blue and beige plaid background clashing with his pristine gray shirt and charcoal slacks. She was sure he'd packed more jeans, but he'd chosen to dress *up* today. That he felt the need to compete with Landry might have given her glee under different circumstances.

Landry, still dressed in the jeans and blue shirt he'd been wearing when he first showed up in her backseat, had claimed a chair directly across from Jeffrey.

The two were silent when she entered the room, but the tension in the air gave her the impression that might not have been the case as recent as mere moments before she arrived.

"I've reached a decision."

Both men turned their attention to her.

"I'll need some time alone with Jeffrey," she said to Landry. This was a private conversation. He knew her history already, there was no reason for him to hang around.

"Not acceptable," Landry countered. "I see no reason to pretend we're not all in this together. Whatever you have to say to one of us, you can say to the other. That's the way it has to be from now on. I've been completely open with you, I expect the same."

His unyielding position on the matter surprised her. She wondered if his about-face had anything to do with whatever words had been exchanged while she was out of the house. Just what she needed, two males attempting to mark their claimed territory.

Arguing would only waste time. "Have it your way."

She sat down on the couch, turning her full attention to Jeffrey. Landry might be determined to listen but that wouldn't keep her from ignoring him. "There's a lot you don't know about me, Jeffrey."

"Evidently."

That he wouldn't look her in the eye roused her suspicions further. Just exactly what had these two been up to?

"Until three years ago," she began again, knowing this would be a hard pill to swallow, "I worked for the CIA."

She had his total interest now. His brow furrowed unnaturally. "The Central Intelligence Agency?"

"Yes. I was a field operative. I rarely stayed in the same place for long. I worked undercover most of the time, using several different identities."

Disbelief started to overtake the confusion that had been lining his face. "What exactly did you do for the CIA?"

Olivia swallowed back the trepidation she abruptly felt pressing against her windpipe and did what had to be done. "I was a black ops assassin."

For about three seconds he merely stared at her then he said, "Really, Olivia, what did you do for them?"

If his voice hadn't been so calm, his expression so expectant, she might have believed he was joking. "I'm telling you the truth, Jeffrey."

"You...killed...people," he suggested, for clarification, it seemed.

Some old habits died hard. Before she realized what she'd done, she found herself looking to Landry for backup. She snatched back her good sense in the nick of time and turned away. "Yes. I killed people."

Jeffrey looked from her to Landry and back. "You're serious?"

"She's telling the truth, Jeffrey."

"I'll handle this." She cut Landry a biting glance. He'd done quite enough already, thank you very much. She didn't need his help, despite her momentary lapse in good sense.

Jeffrey nodded as if he'd decided to consider the events of the past thirty-six or so hours. "So that's what this is all about?" The uncertainty and trepidation in his tone confirmed that he still didn't quite believe her.

"My last assignment was to eliminate a Middle Eastern political figure," she explained. "It was a mistake and that's how I ended up in L.A. starting a new life. My real name is Vanessa Clark." When the truth of her words sank in, he wasn't going to be happy about learning about her past this way. "I'm sorry you got drawn into this situation, but there's nothing I can do about it now."

The realization that she very well could be telling the truth dawned slowly in his eyes.

"You killed people for the CIA."

She nodded.

His gaze swung to Landry's. "Are you CIA, as well?"

"Interpol."

Jeffrey blinked. "This is…" He wagged his head from right to left. "This is unbelievable."

Olivia felt herself relax a bit. At least she'd gotten past that hurdle. "The Company has been out of my life for three years. They thought I was dead. All but Hamilton."

Jeffrey gestured vaguely. "The man whose house you broke into last night?"

She nodded. "He's the deputy director of field operations. When I was active he was my boss. I reported directly to him because of the sensitive nature of my position."

Jeffrey ran a hand through his hair. "You're saying that you killed people for the CIA?"

Apparently that part still hadn't penetrated completely.

"Yes." Clasping her hands in front of her, Olivia took a deep breath and tried again. "Everything I've told you is true. Whether you choose to believe me is up to you, but we have to move on. Our lives depend upon what we do next. Can I count on you?"

Whether it was her persistence that paid off or his own confusion that finally made him relent, he caved. Maybe he just decided that playing along for now was his only choice. That was kind of how she felt about her new partnership with Landry.

"What do you need me to do?"

"I need you to promise me you'll do whatever I ask, no questions, no hesitation."

He looked hesitant already, but he agreed. "All right." He glanced at Landry before settling his gaze on hers once more. "Anything for you, Olivia."

Whatever had transpired between these two had clearly pitted one against the other. That was fine by her. Gave her the edge.

Whatever Landry had planned, he needed to know one thing right now. From this moment on, he was no longer in charge.

She stood. "We have plans to make. Our first step should be determining who all the suspects are. Anyone who had knowledge of the Al Hadi operation, CIA and Interpol." Her gaze lingered on Landry as she spoke. "To do the job right we need a few hours' sleep." She hated to admit that weakness, but she had scarcely slept in days. That kind of handicap would work against her. Sleep deprivation triggered errors in judgment. She'd probably already made one major mistake getting involved with him again. But he'd left her little choice.

Landry pushed to his feet. "That sounds reasonable. Though we shouldn't lose any more time than absolutely necessary."

"Agreed." There was something else she required, as well. "I'll need my weapon and my phone."

Jeffrey rose next. "That goes for me, as well." He

cleared his throat and qualified his statement. "The part about the phone, I mean."

Landry appeared reluctant to meet their demands.

"No negotiations," she spelled out. "We're either equal in this or we go our separate ways."

"As long as you have your end of things under control, I'm good with that."

She didn't have to ask for clarification. He meant Jeffrey. She could handle Jeffrey. Landry handed over her Beretta along with their cell phones.

"It's eight-thirty now," she said after a quick check of the time on her phone's display. "We'll resume this discussion at one."

"I'll see you then."

Landry turned his back and headed down the hall.

He confused her constantly. One minute he had too much to say, the next he had nothing to add.

Nothing about any of this added up, in Olivia's opinion. Particularly Landry's sudden concern for her well-being. Three long years. And now he showed up claiming to want to save her from some imminent doom.

She had absolutely no reason to believe him.

And yet, she wanted to.

Olivia watched the twenty-nine become thirty on the digital clock as the time reached half past noon. She'd slept roughly two hours, and even then she'd awakened every time Jeffrey made the slightest sound or move.

She'd lain there, wide awake, until he dozed off.

He had his phone back and she needed to be sure he didn't use it to call for help. Not that he would want to do anything to injure her, but she felt relatively certain that he considered her certifiable by this point. Despite having been chased, shot at and kidnapped, finding out his significant other was a former assassin couldn't have been easy to take in stride.

She had to be crazy. What was she doing here? How could she trust anything Landry told her?

Olivia sat up and plowed her fingers through her hair. She couldn't. That was the problem. She couldn't trust anyone from her old life.

In some ways she never could. That was part of the game. She played by the rules and she worked under the assumption that the others did, as well. But someone hadn't. That possibility had always been there, lurking just around every corner. It was part of the risk.

She hadn't operated in a vacuum. There had been rumors and rumblings of past betrayals. Agents who were disowned when an op went bad. That protected the Agency. Allowing the agent to take the fall served the greater good. She'd understood that unwritten rule.

But having an agent execute a man whose name hadn't been listed in the book of the dead was wrong any way you looked at it.

Hamilton had given the order.

But someone else had made a mistake.

And she'd paid the price.

Jeffrey didn't rouse as she got up. She tugged on her boots, tucked the knife back into place and tied the laces. The Beretta went into her waistband at the small of her back. She slid her cell into a back pocket.

She hesitated before leaving the room, distracted by her reflection in the mirror above the dresser. She looked tired. She looked nothing like Sheara.

Sheara had been well prepared at all times. Her instincts had been sharp, her skills unmatched. Confidence and relentlessness had exuded from her.

What she saw staring back at her was the fringes of fear and no confidence at all. She fingered the necklace she always wore. Refused to think about the night he'd given it to her.

Olivia closed her eyes. Imagined her long black hair in a chic French twist. A tailored designer suit adorning her five-seven frame. That was Olivia Mills, psychologist.

Vanessa Clark, aka Sheara, was nowhere to be seen.

That one fact was the most dangerous part of what she was about to do.

Sheara could handle anything Landry or anyone else threw her way.

Olivia Mills was soft…compassionate.

She was a dead woman walking if she didn't get her act together.

Her stomach grumbled, signaling that she needed to eat. She'd barely touched her breakfast. She reminded herself that she would need the energy. That was one thing Sheara and Olivia had in common— both were too focused on other things to remember to eat. Great when she was spending hours a day in an elegant leather chair listening to the plight, real or imagined, of a patient. Not so great in survival mode.

As she wandered into the living room, she thought about this house. Landry had said that he'd borrowed it. That could mean several different things, including the possibility that they were here without an invitation. She shook her head. Breaking and entering was the least of her worries right now.

Landry wasn't in the living room or the kitchen. The bathroom door had been standing wide open when she passed and he hadn't been in there, either.

She went to the back door, which was open, and peered beyond the screen door. He stood at the edge of the yard where the trees began. That same boundary she'd likened to her life just a few hours ago.

He stared into the woods a few moments before continuing, following the perimeter where the grass met the trees. Was he ensuring that they were alone out here in the middle of nowhere? Or was he simply killing time?

She pushed the screen door open and walked out onto the porch. She'd reached the last step down to the yard when Landry's attention shifted in her direction. He crossed the yard and met her at the bottom of the steps.

"Are you worried that someone knows we're here?"

"No one knows our location."

She folded her arms over her chest, annoyed that

he could sound so sure. "How can you be certain? We could have been tailed last night."

"We weren't."

Irritation fired her blood. If she were honest with herself she'd have to admit that the part that bothered her most was that he could be so damn certain. That she had once been able to do that and no longer could, evidently, made bad matters worse.

"What about the owner, doesn't he know you're here?"

"No one knows, Nessa."

She stiffened at his use of the nickname only he had used for her.

"Sorry. *Olivia*," he amended.

He wasn't sorry. She read the lie in his eyes.

Maybe her instincts were working better than she'd thought.

"Who owns this place?" She wasn't going to let him get away with all the subterfuge. If they were going to work together she needed everything.

"No one important." He gestured to the door. "We should go inside and discuss our first move."

She held up a hand. "We're not going anywhere until you start giving me the whole story."

His hands braced on his hips, an indicator of his impatience.

Too bad.

"The house belongs to a friend I used to know."

A woman.

The realization struck with startling furor.

"When did you know her?"

"Long before us."

That muscle that always tightened in his jaw when he didn't want to talk about something clenched as she watched.

"How long before us?"

She hadn't meant to ask that. She sounded like a jealous lover. They weren't lovers anymore. Hadn't been for three years. Nothing connected them any longer except a dangerous past that could get them both killed in the next twenty-four hours or less.

"Years."

She had to look away. Couldn't bear the way he looked at her when he said that solitary word. As if he'd suffered…as if he'd cared that he'd lost someone who meant something to him.

Get past it. "So where is she now?"

His shoulders lifted in a show of indifference. "On vacation."

The more questions she asked on the subject, the more interested in his personal life she appeared. That was not the impression she wanted to give. She wasn't interested. She didn't even care.

"So, let's talk." She turned on her heel and went back inside. He followed.

He picked up a folder from the kitchen countertop and joined her at the table.

The folder contained a map, handwritten notes and glossy head shots.

She picked up the first one. "Director Woods."

Olivia had met him on several occasions. Had respected his decisions for the entire seven years she'd worked for the CIA.

The next photo was of Hamilton.

Deputy Director David Hamilton had saved her life. She owed him the benefit of the doubt.

The next head shot was of a staff adviser to the former U.S. president, the one who'd been in the Oval Office when Olivia completed her last assignment for the CIA. This same adviser had, incredibly, moved even higher up the proverbial food chain under the new administration. Men like him always ensured their asses were covered. They knew secrets that could guarantee their passage straight through the Pearly Gates when the time came.

"You think Paul Echols had something to do with this?" She couldn't see it. There were some aspects of the Agency's work that even the president didn't want to know. His adviser would simply use the rule that what he didn't know couldn't hurt him. The odds that he knew the whole story were minimal.

Landry shuffled through his handwritten notes. "Anyone who had access to the orders is a suspect, right?"

Maybe. The final photo was a face she didn't immediately recognize. "Who's this?" The man looked to be about forty or forty-five. Dark hair with a dusting of gray. Steely eyes. He looked aristocratic and somehow vaguely familiar.

"Andrew Page."

"You think your superior was involved?" *Is* involved, she should have said. The idea that Page could be his anonymous source wasn't lost on her. But she would have to depend upon him to supply the possible suspects from Interpol. She could only guess.

"What I said—" he leaned back into his chair "—was that anyone who had access to the orders is a suspect."

She knew what he'd said. She could also read between the lines. "You don't trust Page?" Her impression had always been that the two were close. Had that changed in the past three years?

"That's the question of the hour." He tapped each photo. "Who do we trust?"

Olivia wished he'd taken the time to shave. She blinked, forced her gaze back to the pile of photos. Few men could carry off the look. Unfortunately for her, Landry was one of those chosen few. The coal black whiskers emphasized those planes and angles of his inordinately handsome face that she'd just as soon ignore.

To get herself back on track, she dragged the map to her side of the table. "What do the Xs designate?" He'd drawn a black X in three locations, each surrounded by a square box. A couple of circles, drawn in red ink, highlighted two additional locations. All in the vicinity of Washington, D.C., less than one hundred miles from their current location.

"The Xs are where we can find our suspects for now. I can't guarantee where they'll be twenty-four hours from now. That's why we have to act fast.

This—" he touched one of the red circles "—is our current location. This—" he indicated the other "—is where my former superior is vacationing this week."

"Your *former* superior?" Had she heard wrong?

"Yes."

What the hell? She needed more details. "Andrew Page resigned from Interpol? He was fired? And then he decided to vacation in America?" She'd met Page once or twice. *Debonair* was the one word that summed him up best.

"Neither." Landry shuffled his notes back into the folder. "I quit."

His announcement sent shock waves reverberating through her. "You *left* Interpol?"

"Yes."

Okay, he'd said that. *I quit.* She had to get past the astonishment and get to the facts.

"When? Why?" That information would be immensely helpful for reasons she didn't understand just yet. She couldn't believe it. He'd lived and breathed Interpol.

"Two years ago."

New tremors of shock shuddered through her. This information cast a whole different light on the situation. "How can you possibly have access to the intelligence needed to conduct this operation if you're out of the loop?" He was no better off than she was. What the hell were they doing here? If he was leading them into this blind…

Her gut clenched. Was this further proof that he was an enemy rather than an ally? Stop. She couldn't keep waffling on the issue. She'd made a decision to trust him. If it was a mistake, she'd pay the price in the end. For now, she would operate under the assumption that they were allies.

"I still have my contacts."

But he wasn't looking her in the eye.

"Assuming you're being totally on the up-and-up with me, what's your plan?" She couldn't keep wasting time trying to get him to come clean with her. She reminded herself that keeping certain aspects secret was par for the course. She had, and would do the same.

"We put all the players on alert."

"By reactivating Sheara." He'd set her up to prompt certain responses.

"I needed you to get out of L.A. for your protection. For your friend's, as well. You know they would have used him to get to you."

That she knew.

"I anticipated that you would go to Hamilton. My plan was to rendezvous with you there while Hamilton reacted to your abrupt appearance. Phase one is in motion."

The urge to slug him again welled inside her but she had to hear the rest. He'd set her up and then waited for her to show and she'd done exactly that.

"Now that you've gone to Hamilton," he said, moving on, "he indicated he would start an investigation of his own, yes? What we're looking for is the reaction of others to his actions."

"Every action has a reaction." No doubt about that. "But that doesn't make him the one who fingered me for elimination."

Landry swept the hair back from his forehead with one long-fingered hand. "Let's just say that he's not at the top of my list, either."

She didn't want to notice those kinds of things about him, but her mind kept filtering through the memories of him using those strong hands to touch her. *Focus, Olivia.*

"We can't just sit here and wait for one of these guys to come calling," she countered, chasing away the images. There had to be more to his plan than this.

He watched her closely a moment, most likely to gauge her reaction to what he was about to say. "You're going to pay each one a visit, prod a more aggressive reaction. I'll be your backup."

Before she could respond, he went on, "I wish there was another way. But, unfortunately, it's you they appear to want first and foremost. It has to be you who rattles each cage."

"What am I supposed to offer?"

Those blue eyes stared straight into hers and the answer pierced her heart way before it penetrated her brain. "Me."

Chapter 10

Olivia had a lot more questions for Landry, but there wasn't time.

The game had begun.

Landry placed another piece of tape on the wire tracing a path up the front of her torso. She managed not to shiver this time, which was a major accomplishment since she'd spent the past ten minutes doing just that as he wired her for sound.

"Another sec and we'll be done here." He checked his handiwork and stepped back. "I wish we had wireless but unfortunately this was all I could find on short notice. It's not state-of-the-art but it's top-notch."

Olivia tugged her blouse down and let herself take a much-needed deep breath. That touching her didn't appear to have fazed him made her all the more annoyed with herself.

Jeffrey hadn't stopped pacing since he'd gotten up. Even as he'd nibbled at his lunch, chips and a sandwich, he'd been restless. He was concerned about her. He still thought they should call the authorities.

Landry slipped his earpiece into place. "Let's take her for a test run." He hitched his thumb toward the back door. "Go for fifty yards."

Olivia nodded her agreement and slipped in her own earpiece. Hers was much less conspicuous than Landry's, fitting like a tiny hearing aid.

As soon as Landry left the room, Jeffrey rushed over to her. "Olivia, this is outrageous." His face, his posture, his entire being backed up his assertion. He was scared. For her mostly. "I don't really understand what the two of you hope to accomplish but it sounds very dangerous for you. We should call off this whole thing." He cupped her face with his hands. "As much as it seems I don't know the real you, I don't want you hurt."

"I'll be okay." She took one of his hands in hers. "I've done this hundreds of times." She didn't mention how out of practice she was, since keeping him calm was her goal.

Jeffrey nodded as if he understood, but then resumed pacing around the kitchen. She turned away, stared out the window over the sink as Landry made his way to the edge of the yard.

She'd thought about the truth a few times in the

past three years. Sure, it would have been nice to clear her name. To be free to reclaim her position at the Agency if she so chose. But she'd known something Landry had apparently overlooked. There wasn't any going back. She had a new and completely satisfying career. Why would she want to go back to her old job? She shuddered inwardly at the memories that bobbed to the surface of that ominous lake of history. She worked so hard to keep that dark surface still and calm. Kept all those painful flashes from the past tightly compartmentalized beneath that glassy surface. She couldn't go back. She never wanted to take another life, no matter the cause.

She couldn't be that person anymore. At one time her work had been her calling. She'd felt the passion for serving her country as deeply as anyone who chooses to go into the priesthood. She'd started out as a typical field operative but her ability to infiltrate the enemy, as well as her unparalleled marksmanship, had gotten the Agency's notice. Moving into the position of surgical assassin had been the logical progression.

Heat chased away the icy sensations of resignation as she toyed with the idea that Landry had spoken about more than clearing her name. He'd said that she mattered to him.

He'd watched her from afar all this time. Why hadn't he contacted her sooner? Why let her endure the grief she'd suffered? Didn't he realize how badly the idea that he'd betrayed her had damaged her?

There was a part of her that would never recover from the devastation.

So many questions. Not nearly enough answers.

He was keeping secrets…still. She could feel it. He was going to offer himself as bait, on the premise that he had information they would need. Something, besides the obvious, was totally off here.

"Jeffrey's right, you know."

She tensed as Landry's voice filled her senses.

"This is extremely dangerous," he said. "I'm thinking I should do this alone."

He'd been able to do that before…read her mind.

A new kind of frustration obliterated any aspect of reason she wanted to maintain.

From the corner of her eye she checked on Jeffrey. He'd finally grown weary of pacing and had retired to the sofa. The way he fidgeted, changed positions repeatedly, made her regret all the more palpable.

"Too late for second thoughts now," she said, keeping her voice low enough not to attract Jeffrey's attention. "We don't have a choice."

"I didn't…" He let go a big breath. "I won't let them hurt you again, Nessa. This time I'll have your back the whole distance."

The guilt steeped in his tone echoed in her earpiece, surprising her with its fervor. She fought the powerful sensations that comprehension evoked and ordered herself to focus.

"You never said what you'd been up to for the past

three years." Besides watching her from afar, she didn't add.

"No, I didn't."

That certainly wasn't the answer she'd been digging for. Why the evasiveness? More lies by omission?

She closed her eyes and shook her head in self-disgust. What did she expect? This was the life they had led…before.

"Communications are a go." She wasn't dragging this out any longer than necessary. He wanted to get to her, just like before. And just like before, he wouldn't give as good as he got. She might be a fool but she wasn't totally stupid. Their relationship had always left her desperate for more. She couldn't go there again.

Time to get out of here.

"Jeffrey." She walked into the living room. "We'll be leaving in five minutes. We should gather our things." There was no way to know if they'd be coming back here.

"You're sure you'll be all right with this plan?" he asked again, those brown eyes searching hers for reassurance.

"Sure. This isn't nearly as dangerous as you think."

"Don't lie to him, Nessa."

Olivia jerked the communications piece from her ear and muttered, "Jerk."

Jeffrey, the strap of his bag hefted onto his shoulder, turned to her and frowned. "Hmm?"

She grabbed her overnight bag. "Nothing. I was thinking about Landry."

"I hope this will be over soon," he said as they moved up the hall. "Our neighbors may file a missing person's report. Unlike your friend," he said, pausing for a moment, "we had a life."

Since Landry could hear every word they said via the wire taped to her torso, she imagined that he wouldn't care for the reminder. She had the distinct impression that he didn't like her relationship with Jeffrey. Good. There were a lot of things he'd done that she didn't particularly like. She resisted the urge to tuck the earpiece back into place just to hear what snide remark he might make in response to Jeffrey's comments, but that would be a mistake. The sound of his voice whispering in her ear was far too intimate for her comfort.

They'd loaded their bags into the Land Rover by the time Landry caught up with them. His obvious irritation gave Olivia a refreshing dose of glee.

"We've got plenty of time to check out the situation and get into place." He stowed his bag in the cargo area and went around to the driver's-side door.

Olivia settled into the passenger seat while Jeffrey loaded into the back.

The call to Director Woods had been made.

He was at the top of the suspect list. He had the most power. He wasn't the director of the CIA, but he was the director of field operations. A high-ranking staffer.

It wasn't totally out of the sphere of reality that Hamilton had briefed his superior as well as the special adviser to the president regarding the steps he'd taken to protect Olivia. It just didn't feel right. He would have been risking so much when he could have kept his mouth shut and risked nothing. Had it been necessary for him to get authorization? She didn't know.

She would soon know at least part of the truth. Woods's reaction would tell the tale. She wasn't prepared to label Hamilton as her traitor until she had proof. She'd trusted him for too long. She wasn't naive enough to completely ignore the possibility, but she wasn't going there first.

She'd taken the fall for the CIA three years ago and now they wanted more? Wasn't one life enough to give? That was part of the big mystery. She had to know why her name had suddenly come up again. Why someone suddenly wanted her dead again.

If Woods was the one...

She'd do what? Shoot him? Slug him?

Watching Landry in her peripheral vision, her respiration reacted to the emotions churning inside her.

She couldn't go into the operation like this. Control was key.

If they could stop whoever wanted her dead, maybe they could prove she was innocent of the accusations she'd had thrown at her three years ago.

The idea of clearing her name brought with it a calming effect. Maybe she did deserve to have her name cleared...to have her life back if she wanted it.

The Agency had done this to her and Landry had

let it happen. That was the bottom line. Maybe he was back now out of some belated sense of guilt. She just didn't care. She had to find out who the hell had started this new threat to her and find a way to end it. She had to protect Jeffrey. He was the one who didn't deserve any of this. If she were lucky enough to clear her name in the process, well, that was great.

Better than great.

She focused on the burn of anger. She needed that heat to fuel her Sheara persona. When she was angry was the only time she felt any sort of connection to the person she used to be.

That connection might very well be the only thing that stood between her and certain death.

Her gaze shifted fully to the driver and she looked away just as quickly. She'd counted on him once and he'd let her down. Would this time be different?

As much as she didn't want to admit it, she needed him for this. They couldn't fail.

The people who had held the power over her past were about to learn that Vanessa Clark wouldn't be so damn easy to kill twice.

The rendezvous point was the Springfield Mall, only a few minutes from the nation's Capitol. The food court would have been too obvious. She'd chosen the Victoria's Secret store instead.

To ensure Woods didn't set a trap for her, he wasn't apprised of the exact location of the meet until he arrived on-site at 4:00 p.m.

This was the moment of truth. What high-ranking CIA official would put himself through the paces for a ghost from the past? If Woods showed, she would know without doubt that this was big. She would know that it wasn't over as she'd thought for three years.

Olivia picked through a rack of silky lingerie as she covertly watched the front entrance to the store. Landry and Jeffrey were stationed on a bench only five or six yards outside the entrance. Landry wore an iPod on his belt to cover for the earpiece, which was considerably more noticeable than the one she had slipped into her ear. A New York Yankees ball cap camouflaged his face to some degree. Jeffrey sat on the other end of the bench, appearing engrossed in a hardback from the bookstore two stores down.

Landry would listen to the conversation and jump in to back her up if necessary.

Olivia had already checked out the dressing area as well as the employee exit in the rear. A fast getaway wouldn't be a problem.

"Heads up."

Her hand missed the next hanger as Landry's voice reverberated softly in her ear.

"The target has arrived," he warned.

Adrenaline roared like a fire through her veins. Olivia studied a lovely turquoise silk gown. "I see him," she murmured.

He was there.

CIA Field Operations Director Arvin Woods entered the lingerie shop alone. But he wouldn't be alone. It didn't take a lot of imagination to figure out several of the patrons loitering in the spacious corridor outside the shop were probably undercover agents serving as his personal security and backup.

She maintained her position as he crossed to an adjacent rack of sexy nightwear and started to sift through the glamorous items, feigning interest.

Taking her time, she sized up the man she had not seen in three years. She remembered when he accepted the position eight years ago at age thirty-nine, the youngest director in the Agency's history. His blond hair no doubt required help to stay that way these days. The tan hadn't come from lying on the beach. The suit likely sported a designer label and a hefty price tag. He looked well, hadn't really aged. Not like Hamilton. She imagined the major shit ran downhill. The deputy director wound up taking the heat more often than the director himself.

The possibility that she might have been his scapegoat sent a new surge of outrage roaring through her. The realization that he was here solely because she had called and asked him to be was all the proof she needed that Landry had told her the truth.

She moved to a table where delicate thongs were stacked in mounds of mint green, baby blue, girlie pink and virgin white. She felt the director's scrutiny on her but she didn't let the attention make her nervous. He wanted to be sure it was her before he approached.

Her hair was darker and longer than before. She'd stayed in shape out of habit more so than desire. Now she was glad she'd stuck with her workouts.

He walked in her direction, fingered the lacy edge of a pink thong as he paused at the table.

"Hello, Miss Clark."

"Director Woods."

"I'm sure you'll understand when I say I thought you were dead."

"I was." She met that analyzing gray gaze. "Until someone resurrected me."

He picked up the panties that appeared to strike his fancy, shifted his attention to the sexy feminine textures as he spoke. "Hamilton will certainly have some explaining to do."

He sounded sincere. No way, however, would she assume he hadn't known just because he said so. Sadly, no one did that anymore. At least not in this business.

"Hamilton did what he had to do to protect his agent."

Those gray eyes bored into hers. "He lied to his superior. He allowed the Agency to believe you were dead and an international incident of significant proportions went unresolved as a result."

"The explanation is simple," she told him without hesitation. "I was set up to take the fall for someone else's scheme. Now I want my life back. I want my name cleared. I want you to make that happen for me."

He selected the baby blue panties to go along with the pink ones he'd already picked up. "I can assure you, Vanessa, if you were wronged I will make it right. To do that, however, I'll need your full cooperation." He settled his full attention back on her. "We need to finally clear up the mess that happened three years ago. You can help us do that. But I can't help you if you aren't willing to come in."

Like she would do that. *Come in* was spookspeak for give yourself up. No way was she going down that path. Hamilton had saved her from that fate several years ago and she wasn't about to get caught in that trap now.

"In that case, I'll take my chances on my own."

"If that's your decision, I'm afraid I won't be able to support your endeavor, Miss Clark."

She picked up a pair of mint green panties as well as a pair of white ones and passed them to him. "Buy three get one free."

"Don't make this mistake, Miss Clark," he cautioned firmly. "It could have devastating consequences. Whatever you and Hamilton arranged three years ago is clearly no longer valid. You'll lose whatever life you've managed to salvage these last three years. Is that what you want?"

"I've already lost it." Keeping the bitterness out of her tone was impossible. "Besides, I have backup this time."

"I'm not sure what that means, Miss Clark."

"Holt Landry is prepared to confirm everything I say. If you can't help me, then we'll just have to go to the media." She studied him closely, didn't want to miss the slightest shift in his expression or his posture as he absorbed her blatant threat. If he was guilty she wanted to read it on his face, in his eyes or in his voice.

"Threatening me won't help you, Miss Clark. I cannot measure the relativity of what you're trying to say. I've offered my help. What you do from here is your choice."

She wanted to believe he was manipulating her, but there was no outward indication, no subtle change in the tone of his voice or indicative physical manifestations of deceit. Then again, like her, he knew all the tricks. He could be lying. But if she only had what she saw and heard upon which to judge his sincerity, she would have to say he was telling the truth.

"In that case, this meeting is over."

He sighed. His hands found the edge of the table as if he needed the extra support to stay vertical. "My offer stands, Miss Clark. Think long and hard before you betray the Agency or your country."

That he would throw a blow that low infuriated her all the more. "Considering I eliminated a target that shouldn't have been a target because the Agency ordered me to, I'd say *my* loyalty has never been in question." Emotion welled in her voice, betraying her resolve. Dammit.

"That decision was not mine." His gaze pressed in on hers once more. "The order came straight from the president. However badly you want to clear your name, Miss Clark, you have to know the likelihood of that happening in a public forum is very low. Going to the media with information you can't officially substantiate will only harm you."

"So you've wasted your time as well as mine with this little discussion." She laughed softly. "I was certain a man as busy as yourself doesn't have that kind of time to waste."

"Come in with me, Miss Clark, and we'll work this out. You have my word."

"No, thanks."

He squared his shoulders, the elegant blue silk suit regal against the crisp white of his shirt and the power-red tie he wore. "In that case, there's nothing I can do for you. Good luck, Miss Clark."

She watched him walk out of the store, the panties he'd considered buying left in a crumpled heap on the table.

"You okay?"

Landry.

"Yeah."

"I'm going to follow him out. Make sure he leaves without talking to anyone else. Then I'll make my way over to the Land Rover. You and Jeffrey meet me there in five minutes."

Through the glass front of the shop she watched Landry fall into step a few yards behind the director, his baseball cap pulled low. Jeffrey got up from the bench and wandered into the shop to join her.

"I assume things didn't go the way you'd hoped."

He frowned at the rumpled panties the director had left behind. Jeffrey liked things neat.

"Too early to tell." She glanced at her watch. "Let's go. We'll need to make sure we don't have any tails before we meet Landry."

This whole thing could turn out to be a bust. Director Woods appeared to have no idea what she was talking about. If he hadn't been in on the plan, then that left Hamilton on the CIA side of things. Had the president sanctioned that final assignment or had he simply looked the other way? There was Paul Echols, the president's top adviser at the time. And of course, Andrew Page, the Interpol counterpart. The operation couldn't have gone down the way it did without one or more of them knowing the facts.

It didn't matter as much who knew as who made the final decision. That was the real answer she needed. Then she would know why her life expectancy continued to be far too short.

Since an emergency egress didn't seem necessary, she and Jeffrey moved into the mall's main thoroughfare and headed toward the food-court entrance. Just another part of all this that didn't make sense. Why let her walk away? Now or three years ago? And what about last night? Hamilton hadn't made any move to stop her. He'd known she was alive all this time. Why let her sit idle for three years? Why not act before now? What had changed?

There had to be more to this than Landry was telling her. Maybe more than he knew.

If she found out he'd left her in the dark and let her walk into this tête-à-tête blind, she would kick his...

As they passed the carousel loaded with delighted children, an electrical charge zapped along her nerve endings, making the tiny hairs on the back of her neck stand on end.

"Jeffrey."

He stopped, only then realizing that she was no longer beside him. "Is something wrong?"

Olivia prodded herself forward—she didn't dare turn around. "We're going to take a little detour."

He looked at his watch. "We only have three minutes until we're supposed to meet Landry. We really should be on our way."

A long-ago deeply ingrained instinct sent adrenaline charging through her veins. She grabbed Jeffrey by the arm and started forward again.

"Listen to me, I won't have time to say this twice."

"I'm listening." He leaned his head closer to hers as they continued to weave quickly through the meandering Sunday-afternoon shopping crowd. "What's going on, Nessa?"

Shit. She'd forgotten about Landry and the wire.

"I think we have a tail."

"You think or you know?"

Damn him. Didn't he get it? She'd been out of this business for three years. She wasn't sure.

Frustrated, she stopped and turned around. The

abrupt moves of no less than three *shoppers* some four or five yards behind her gave her the answer she sought.

"I fucking know, Landry."

He swore the way Brits will do when annoyed. Politely, with arrogant dignity.

"Get the hell out of there," he ordered. "I'll be waiting for you at the curb."

Nothing polite or dignified about that.

If they made a dead run for it the chase would begin.

She scanned the upcoming shops. The food-court entrance was near one of the anchor stores…Macy's. They still had a ways to go to get there.

They needed to lose this tail.

She looped her arm through Jeffrey's. "We have to move quickly, Jeffrey. Just stay with me, okay?"

His arm tightened around hers. "I'm right beside you."

She would owe him big-time when this was over… assuming they survived.

She cut into the candy store on the right. The shop was packed with patrons, which helped. She tugged Jeffrey through the crowd and exited on the opposite side of the store. This time she wasn't walking, she was running.

"Talk to me, Nessa."

Why the hell didn't he stop calling her that?

Hanging on to Jeffrey's hand, she rushed into Macy's. The only way to stay ahead of the man behind her was to move through a crush of shoppers. The guys on her tail would have the same training as her. Losing them in an open area would be next to impossible.

"Answer me, Nessa, or I'm coming in."

"We're on our way, Landry."

She cut through the men's department. Wished like hell she knew where the employee exits were located.

The guy in the jeans, T-shirt and sneakers was gaining on them. They had to move faster. Yet attracting unnecessary attention wouldn't be a good thing.

Dammit.

She headed for the women's department. Her heart rocketed into her throat. She couldn't let them catch her. Not now, with Jeffrey stuck in the middle.

The sign for the dressing room captured her attention. She dashed in that direction. Was immensely grateful no clerks were close by as she pushed through the stylish curtain providing privacy as well as elegance to the entrance.

Thankfully Jeffrey didn't put up any resistance as she urged him deeper into what he would consider forbidden territory.

She pushed him into one of the larger, handicapped-accessible dressing rooms and latched the door. She pressed her finger to her lips to signal silence to him, then pointed to the bench. He nodded and scooted onto the bench, his knees pulled up to his chest to prevent his feet from being seen beneath the door.

Olivia shucked her boots and jeans, tossed both onto the bench with Jeffrey. Fortunately for her, the previous occupant had left a dress and a pair of slacks in the room. She jumped into the slacks that were two sizes too large but she didn't care. The dress she hung over the door so that anyone who approached on the other side would think she was a customer trying on clothes.

She fiddled with the skirt of the dress, making just enough noise to sound as if she was preparing to try on another outfit.

Holding her breath, she listened for the enemy's approach. She knew better than to hope he'd give up so easily. Or that her maneuver had been so brilliant.

A rap on the door directly in front of her sent her pulse into Mach speed.

Her body went rigid in preparation to fight.

"Did the dress work, ma'am?"

Relief made her sway on her feet.

Salesclerk.

Olivia moistened her lips and summoned her voice. "Could you bring me a size smaller, please?"

"Certainly. I'll be right back."

Olivia pressed her forehead against the door and tried to catch her breath. Damn, that had been close. But they weren't out of here yet. She glanced at Jeffrey, who looked just a little nervous.

She needed to know if her tail was close by.

"Nessa, where are you now?"

Landry. He was supposed to back her up. He wasn't doing her a damn bit of good with him out there and her in here. But then, if he were in here he'd only be trapped the same as she was.

She exhaled a long blast of air.

Before she could answer him, the salesclerk re-appeared and rapped on the door again. "Here you go, ma'am."

Uncertain if this was the right risk to take, Olivia opened the door just far enough to reach out. The salesclerk smiled and passed the dress to her.

"Excuse me." Olivia's voice cracked in spite of her best efforts to keep it level.

The salesclerk turned back to her, a questioning look on her face.

"There's a man—" Olivia wet her lips again "—my ex-boyfriend. He's been following me around the mall. I think he's out there waiting for me." Landry would hear the conversation and understand that she had a plan. She hoped.

The clerk looked distressed. "Would you like me to call security?"

Olivia shook her head, summoned her deepest, darkest fear for motivation. "That'll only make him more angry. He knows where I live."

"What does he look like?" The clerk looked ticked off now. Clearly she had no tolerance for men who stalked their ex-girlfriends.

"Tall, brown hair, jeans, blue T-shirt."

She nodded, her expression knowing. "Oh, yes, he's out there. He tried to come in here but I stopped him. And there's another man with him."

Olivia rounded her eyes. "What will I do? I need to get to my car and get away from him."

The clerk thought about that for a moment. "Where is your car parked?"

"Near the food-court entrance."

She pursed her lips, then nodded resolutely. "I can take you out the back entrance." She gestured behind her. "There's a storeroom back there where incoming shipments are received and checked in."

Olivia marshaled a look of desperate hope. "That would be great."

The clerk hesitated, making Olivia's heart ram against her breastbone.

"Do you want the dress?" she asked.

Damn. "Of course. How much is it?"

The clerk looked at the sales ticket. "Two-fifty plus tax."

"Just a moment." Olivia drew back from the door and looked to Jeffrey.

Momentarily bewildered, understanding kicked in before Olivia had a chance to panic. He wrenched his wallet from his back pocket and dragged out a platinum Visa. She shook her head adamantly. Comprehension dawned and this time he drew out three one-hundred-dollar bills. His hand shook as he passed the cash to Olivia.

She would make this up to him. Somehow.

After giving the money to the clerk, she urged, "Please hurry."

The clerk smiled and folded the dress over her

arm. "Don't worry. I'll be right back. The door's just over there." She pointed to the storeroom access. "I'll have you out of here before he knows what hit him."

Olivia nodded, managing a faint smile of her own.

When the clerk had disappeared beyond the curtain that blocked anyone outside from looking in, Olivia stripped off the slacks. She jerked on her jeans and shoved her feet into her boots, arranged the knife to a comfortable position and decided to forgo lacing the ties.

She put her mouth to Jeffrey's ear. "I'm going to check that door to see if it's locked. If it's not, we're out of here."

He frowned. "What if the clerk comes back?"

"I'll tell her we got spooked and decided to leave without the dress."

He nodded, didn't bring up the three hundred bucks she'd just thrown away.

Olivia checked the corridor outside the dressing rooms. Clear. Leaving the door open, she moved to the end of the corridor as quickly and silently as she could.

Her fingers closed around the cool metal knob of the door the clerk had indicated. Olivia gave the knob a twist, her heart beating so loudly she could scarcely hear herself think.

The knob didn't resist and the latch released. She pushed the door inward and found the storeroom the clerk had told her about.

Jeffrey watched from the dressing-room door. She motioned for him to come. He hurried toward her, while she watched the curtain at the other end of the corridor.

Once he was inside the storeroom she closed the door, careful not to make any unnecessary noise.

A lit exit sign reigned over the door that would provide their escape. Relief made her light-headed.

"This way." She grabbed Jeffrey's hand and hurried toward the rear exit.

She pushed the door open and a shadow blocked the sun that should have greeted her.

Her gaze collided with triumphant brown eyes.

The third man who'd been following her.

Damn.

Chapter 11

The first thing Olivia noticed about the man blocking her escape was that he hadn't drawn his weapon.

The second thing was that he hadn't expected Jeffrey.

The precious seconds it cost him to analyze the other man's threat level was the opportunity Olivia needed.

Her right knee rushed toward his family jewels, but he wasn't that distracted. He twisted. Grabbed her by the shoulders in an attempt to pin her to the door.

She jerked free, landed an uppercut to his chin. He grabbed a handful of hair and shoved her back into the storeroom.

Before she regained her balance, he was filling the doorway and reaching for his weapon.

An arm came down hard on the guy's head. Olivia had to look twice to make sure she'd seen what she thought she saw. Jeffrey had ripped an arm from a mannequin and slammed the guy with it.

Though rattled, the guy still lunged for Jeffrey. Olivia's left elbow collided with his temple as the two went down.

Jeffrey shoved the motionless body off him and scrambled to his feet. Olivia grabbed his arm and ran like hell.

The Land Rover skidded to a stop at the curb two seconds before she reached it.

Landry shoved the passenger-side door open. "Get in!"

Like she needed an invitation. She flung herself into the front seat. Jeffrey dived into the back. Landry was barreling across the parking lot before their doors were fully closed.

Olivia didn't have to look back to know they were being followed. Landry's risky maneuvers around pedestrians and parked vehicles screamed trouble on his heels.

"Try not to get us or anyone else killed, Landry," Jeffrey shouted above the alternating sounds of squealing tires and screeching brakes. The click of his seat belt punctuated his anxious statement.

"We need to get to the street." Olivia watched for a break in the lines of traffic bottlenecked at both the exits within visual range. The thoroughfares around the mall didn't give them the freedom they needed to get off mall property. But maneuvering around the throng of waiting vehicles would be no easy feat.

"Keep an eye out for cops." Landry's determined expression told her he had a plan.

She craned her neck right then left, didn't see any official cruisers. Landry didn't wait for her assessment. He bumped over the curb where the thoroughfare circling the mall met the landscape. If there were any cops around they would soon know.

Olivia braced herself.

Landry veered around the Springfield Mall sign and cut into the street right in front of merging traffic.

Horns blared. Tires squealed as brakes were slammed.

A black SUV carrying at least one member of her original tail followed, bouncing onto the pavement and cutting off more outraged drivers.

Landry swooped between cars and roared along turning lanes, leaving furious drivers and the occasional fender bender in his wake, in an effort to put some distance between them and the vehicle determined to keep theirs in sight.

He didn't slow. Not for a second. Not for anything.

Olivia found herself holding her breath more than once. Each time the crash didn't come she sucked in a thankful breath. It had been a while since she'd taken a ride anything like this, even on L.A.'s infamous freeways. Distracting the driver with unnecessary questions or comments wouldn't help.

Landry did what he had to do.

The exit for I-95 didn't come soon enough for Olivia. She exhaled a fraction of her tension as he zoomed up the ramp. The tail was still hanging on, but it would be a hell of a lot easier to lose him once they could pick up some real speed.

Weaving and darting between and around vehicles, Landry managed to get in the right position to whip off onto an exit before his tail could react to the abrupt move. He missed the turn, would have no choice but to go to the next exit and double back.

Landry slowed marginally but didn't let up on his evasive maneuvers. By the time he stopped taking unexpected turns, even Olivia was lost. She'd spent her share of time in the D.C. area and popular surrounding locales, but she was pretty sure she'd never been here before.

"Where to now?" she asked when it was safe to distract Landry. She had more questions and conclusions. The sooner they were off the road the sooner they could assess what just went down.

"Anywhere," Jeffrey pleaded. "I just want to get out of this vehicle."

Olivia couldn't bring herself to look at him. She'd put him in this position. He wanted to go home. He wanted his life back.

She hated herself right now.

Her gaze shifted to the man behind the wheel.

Maybe she still hated him, too. But not nearly enough to protect herself.

More than an hour and a half later Landry stopped at a hotel off the Capital Beltway. As distance went, they hadn't actually gone that far from their rendezvous point with Director Woods, but they'd been driving hard the entire time.

Olivia understood the tactic. Ensure the enemy couldn't pick up your trail. The dude who'd been hoping to catch them would need a crystal ball to do so now.

Landry had doubled back so many times he'd driven twenty miles for every five he wanted to cover. There had been no sign of the black SUV since they'd left I-95.

That was definitely a good thing.

Landry parked the Land Rover near the entrance to the hotel lobby. He looked exhausted. Somehow she didn't feel sorry for him though. After all, he'd started this.

"How about getting us a couple of rooms with a connecting door." He handed her a credit card.

He looked away before she could read his eyes, but she'd noticed something there…that distant look of remorse or something along those lines. Couldn't be. That would indicate he had a heart and she knew from experience he didn't. Not one any human could hope to reach anyway.

She had to stop trying to read between the lines. What he thought or how he felt was of no consequence to her any longer. Not on that level. They were partners in an op, that was all.

Not bothering to answer him, she got out of the SUV and went to do his bidding. Her legs felt a little wobbly. She'd lived the calm, safe life too long to go through a high-speed chase without feeling it.

Inside, the desk clerk greeted her and in less than three minutes had taken care of her request. Two rooms, connecting door, third floor. Nothing on the ground floor was available. She used the credit card he'd given her. Samuel Borders, one of his many aliases.

"Three seventy and seventy-one," she informed Landry as she climbed back into the Land Rover.

He drove around to the end of the hotel and parked out of sight of the main entrance. He didn't bother to back into the slot as she'd done in Memphis.

Landry claimed his bag from the cargo area. Olivia and Jeffrey did the same. She was beginning to worry about him. He hadn't said a word since they left I-95.

That communication strike ended the instant she and Jeffrey were alone in their own room.

"Olivia, we have to contact the police. This is way, way out of control." He dropped his bag onto the bed and rubbed a hand over his face. He looked haggard. Clearly he had reached the end of his rope emotionally.

She couldn't keep lugging him around with her. He could have been killed today.

They both could have.

The reality that she hadn't drawn her weapon when coming face-to-face with the enemy scared her more than any other aspect of the day's adventure.

Why hadn't her survival instincts kicked in?

She should have had her weapon in her hand before she opened that door. Her enemy's failure to draw his own weapon was the only thing that had saved her ass.

As well as Jeffrey's.

And it didn't make a damn lick of sense.

Jeffrey sat down on the edge of the bed. His somber face warned Olivia that she might not be talking him out of his decision this time.

"If you choose to leave this hotel with Landry then you'll be doing so alone," he said flatly. "I can't go along with this any longer."

She sat down next to him. "I'm sorry you got dragged into this, Jeffrey." Clasping her hands in her lap, she let her shoulders sag with her own fatigue. "I don't know what's going to happen. The only thing I'm certain of at this point is that I can't walk away."

"It's his fault." He glared toward the connecting door she had yet to unlock. "He started this mess."

She couldn't argue either of those statements, not really. What she could do was ask some more questions. The reactions of Woods and his men had given her pause.

"I need to speak with him." She searched Jeffrey's face for signs of disapproval. "Will you be okay over here for a few minutes? You won't make any calls until I get back and we've talked?"

"No calls until you come back. But I don't trust him," he said firmly. "Be careful what you agree to. I'm certain he has some hidden agenda that will only create more trouble for you."

She stood. "I'll be back soon."

Jeffrey massaged the back of his neck. "I think I'll order room service or takeout if that's okay."

"Sure." She hesitated at the door. "Don't forget the Pepsi." Somehow she managed to dredge up a smile. "Be right back."

She opened the doors leading to Landry's room without knocking. He would be expecting her. He'd left his side unlocked. There would be no question in his mind what she was thinking. He'd heard the conversation between her and the director.

Landry had stripped down to his jeans. She reminded herself not to visually examine his well-defined chest. She'd seen it before. No need to linger there. She knew every amazing contour.

"I still feel like you're keeping something from me, Landry." Why beat around the bush? He had to be expecting this. She closed the door behind her. Some aspects of this conversation were off-limits to Jeffrey…could actually endanger him even further.

"I told you everything I can."

Landry kicked back on the bed, the pillows behind him for support as he reviewed his map.

The desire to whip out her Beretta and make him talk was palpable. The only problem with that scenario was that she could shoot out his kneecaps and he still wouldn't talk. Not unless he wanted to. That part she knew for sure.

She assumed a position next to the bed, adopting her most intimidating posture. "Woods had no idea what I was talking about. He had no idea I was alive. I just can't figure out if that's related to what you're not telling me."

He set his map aside and pushed to his feet, forcing her to take two steps back to avoid his entering her personal space. "You can't be certain of anything yet, Nessa. Woods may have told you what he wanted you to hear."

Tiny blasts of annoyance imploded, one by one, deep inside her. He did that, used her old name, just to keep her off balance.

Unfortunately it worked.

"I saw his face, Landry. Saw his eyes. He wasn't lying. I really want to believe that you're not."

He moved closer. Too close. The implosions of irritation turned to anticipation. Her pulse responded.

"I need you to trust me a little longer," he said, his tone too low, too intimate for comfort.

She firmed her defenses, held her ground. He wasn't going to influence her with his vast charm. "I still say he didn't know."

"We're not finished yet. There's still Hamilton and Echols."

"What about Andrew Page?" she demanded. "Is your former Interpol superior suddenly exempt?"

Somehow he was closer now. She'd scarcely blinked and he'd invaded her territory. She hadn't noticed him move, but that bare chest felt too close...too inviting.

"Woods might not have been the one," Landry allowed, "but he turned a blind eye when you went down. Whether he knew the specifics of your situation or not, he understood that something wrong happened. Andrew isn't exempt, either. He knows things...the same as the others do. The bottom line is, whatever Woods did or did not know, he wanted to take you in today. That much was clear. We can't let up until we've got them all running in circles."

She backed up a step. She didn't care if he recognized his effect on her. She couldn't stand there feeling the heat from his body a second longer.

"Nothing we do is going to clear my name," she countered. "Vanessa Clark is dead. She died a rogue agent, a traitor. End of story, Landry. No matter if we prove who gave the order, the woman I used to be will still be dead and buried. We need to stick to a single agenda—finding out who wants Olivia Mills dead."

For the third time since he'd crashed back into her life she failed to see his next move coming. His fingers were suddenly in her hair, tugging her close... his mouth claimed hers in an act so bold, so demanding that she couldn't assemble a proper thought much less an evasive maneuver.

He kissed her the way he had before, with every ounce of his being. She didn't have to wonder...she could feel all of him in the act. Holt Landry was a master kisser...an equally masterful lover. She shuddered, tried not to think.

He pulled back just far enough to draw in a desperate breath, the rush of air between their damp lips sending fire raging through her.

"God, I've missed you."

The words...his touch...were too much.

She planted her palms against that bare chest and pushed with what meager strength he hadn't drained from her. "Don't do this."

He wouldn't let her go. He held on, cradling her face in his hands. "Do you know what it did to me when I thought you were dead? I couldn't sleep. I couldn't eat. Couldn't work. Nothing. I searched for you. Talked to a thousand people in an attempt to confirm what I'd been told. I was crazy with grief." He pressed his forehead to hers. Stroked her cheek with his thumb. "I couldn't bear the idea that you were gone."

She pushed harder against him. Had to get some distance between them. The desire to touch him more intimately…to have him skin to skin was almost overwhelming.

She was a fool. A damn fool. How the hell could she still feel this way knowing what she knew about their past? She couldn't let him change the subject like this.

"They took you from me." He backed off a little but he didn't let go completely. His hands rested on her shoulders, maintaining the connection that was tearing her apart inside. "They destroyed all that you were. I want them to pay. I want the people responsible to face up to their crimes. I want you safe."

It would be so easy to believe him. So simple to fall into his arms and take up right where they left off three years ago.

But things were too complicated right now…and even if they weren't, how could she trust her heart to him again? Nothing he said, no amount of scorching kisses, would change the facts. He'd damaged her too badly.

"I need the truth, Landry. The whole truth."

His hands fell away and she hoped the resignation in his eyes was real. There could be no more secrets between them…not about this.

"You're right." Landry shoved his hands into his pockets, emphasizing the part of him that had once given Olivia great pleasure. "I haven't told you everything."

She felt weak with relief. "Tell me." She inhaled

a shaky breath. "Tell me everything. I have to know all of it."

"Somehow someone found out you were still alive. We don't know who it is yet, but whoever it is, he wants you dead."

Frustration furrowed its way across her brow. "Why? What is it they think I know?"

"You're the only one left who knows what really happened. Even I wasn't there when the assassination went down. No matter the threats we toss around, alone, anything I say will only be chalked up to hearsay or conjecture. But you were there. You carried out the hit. Your testimony combined with my statement would nail someone's ass to the wall."

"That administration is over," she protested. "Mistakes that were made three years ago will only be seen as a nuisance and swept under the rug. I'm betting our new president wouldn't be that worried about what I did then. Regardless of what's going on in the Middle East." Though the media's ability to twist ancient history into current events could make a person deeply regret an action, past or present. There was that, she supposed.

"Under normal circumstances you would be right," he assented.

He rested his hands at his waist, the muscles of his arms flexing and contracting with the move, disrupting her focus as well as her respiration. She needed him to get to the point. Spending any more time with him in this suggestive setting was asking for trouble.

"Remember I told you that old enemies were now allies."

"Of course." She watched the news. Anywhere you looked there was trouble brewing. Great care was required to keep the delicate balance even among those political venues this government had once snubbed.

"If word gets out that someone in the American government had such an important man killed for no other reason than to influence an election, that someone will be done in this business. No one knows, outside the handful of suspects we've talked about and the two of us, that the CIA was responsible for that assassination, Vanessa. If the man who gave that order is exposed, he'll be lucky to walk away with his life. But worst of all, relations with the Middle East will be shattered, regardless of whether the current administration is innocent or not."

The scariest part of his ongoing monologue was that he was absolutely right. She had sensed that he'd known more than he was telling—now she knew for certain.

"Perception is everything these days," he persisted. "All it takes is one black mark to push a player out of the game. Our president doesn't want any additional trouble in the Middle East. Particularly considering the country whose leader you took out of action has now formed an alliance not only with the U.S. but with former ruthless enemies. Enemies with whom the U.S.

has waited decades to negotiate. A historical alliance will soon be under way. The administration can't afford any ripples. My guess is that your old mission was brought up within the context of possible stumbling blocks and someone has decided that he needs to tie up any remaining loose ends to ensure he isn't sorry later."

In other words, despite being dead as far as the Agency was concerned, she had become a liability.

"Why didn't you just give me a call and tell me this in the first place?" Frustration and fury overtook the suspicion and surprise, making her madder than hell. "Why the game?"

"I received word that you'd been targeted for elimination. I was afraid you wouldn't listen to me and I was right. You wouldn't have. I had to do something drastic to get your attention so you'd act quickly."

She went toe-to-toe with him, no longer concerned with keeping her distance or how he looked or how he smelled. "And just how did you come to have access to this information, Mr. Landry, ex–Interpol agent?" He'd told her he'd quit. How could he be this deeply involved with this operation—and that was exactly what this was—and be retired, so to speak?

He looked away. A concession to guilt?

"Who is your source, Landry?" She couldn't be here if he didn't tell her everything. He was in this up to his eyeballs, dammit.

"My former superior."

Andrew Page had set this whole thing in motion. Why? She moved in closer still. "Look at me when you speak to me, Landry. I want to see the lie in your eyes."

As if in slow motion his face turned back to hers; their gazes connected and she wasn't prepared for what she saw.

Pain…fear.

Impossible.

She blinked.

Landry had never been afraid of anything.

He had no heart. He couldn't feel pain or fear.

"I watched you all that time. Wanted you." He licked his lips, the lingering taste of their kiss no doubt still there. His voice weaving a spell even now she couldn't resist. "But I stayed away," he confessed softly, "to protect you. I wouldn't risk endangering you. Alone you were invisible, but the two of us would have been too risky."

The spell he cast so easily shattered as she reminded herself that he hadn't been there to back her up when she'd needed him three years ago. Fury ate a path through her chest. "To protect me? How the hell were you protecting me? You were the reason I had to agree to faking my own death, you son of a bitch!"

She clamped her mouth shut. Forced herself to take a breath. If she started yelling again, Jeffrey would come to check on her. He didn't need to hear any of this.

"I took on the CIA, Nessa," Landry admitted, his tone still quiet and calm, frustratingly so.

She let her glare speak for itself. "What does that mean?"

"I raised hell. Let them know that I knew what they'd done. Andrew was the only reason I was able to walk away from the confrontation. He took immediate action. Got me out of the country. Probably saved my life."

Her stomach dropped to her toes. "You were targeted for elimination because of what you knew."

He nodded. "I was just like you. I had to disappear to stay alive."

A whole load of emotions dumped on her at once. He'd lost his life as well because of that operation. He'd gone through the same thing she had.

Her breath caught. "What about your mother?"

He shook his head. "I couldn't risk seeing her or even calling her."

Olivia's hand when to her throat. That was the one part of Landry that had always grounded him in the human race, the way he doted about his mother. "She must miss you terribly."

His gaze shifted away from her again. "She died last year."

Olivia closed her eyes and forced back the emotions pounding at her brain. She had to think. Had to process all this information.

Damn whoever had done this to them.

"I'm working as a go-between. Andrew trusts me. He'll listen to me. We have to know who is responsible. It's the only way we'll ever make this right," he said, his gaze leveling on hers once more. "Hamilton fits near the top of that category."

"I'm not willing to lay this on him just yet." She rubbed her right temple, a headache beginning there. She needed to eat. As if she'd only just awoken from a long sleep, the smell of the pizza Jeffrey had ordered wafted beneath the door and tugged at her senses.

"But…" When she set aside personal feelings and really considered Hamilton as a suspect, she just couldn't get past the idea that he would have let her live for three years only to suddenly want her dead. "If it's Hamilton, why didn't he eliminate me before?"

"My understanding is that this new political arrangement only recently became a priority, making this dirty little secret suddenly a far more volatile issue."

She shook her head. "Then why didn't he kill me the other night when he had the chance? I walked right into his weekend home. He had the perfect opportunity."

"That one's simple."

She waited expectantly for him to explain what was so damn simple about it.

"He needs both of us dead. He was waiting for me to show up. You know, kill two birds with one stone. If he had eliminated you too quickly he would have risked any chance of reeling me in. He wouldn't have found me in a million years."

Jesus. That part could definitely be true. That still didn't convince her that Hamilton was dirty.

"But why have me tell Woods that you were going to back me up if you were already on his hit list?"

"Our goal is to find the truth. To ferret out just how high up the chain of command the betrayal goes. The only way to do that is to use the element of surprise. Shock value. Make them think we know more than we do. That's what you accomplished with Woods today. Now we'll see what Woods does with this new information. He knows we're together and that we've formed a plan of action. He didn't want us to get away but we did. Now he has no choice but to react."

"We're giving each suspect the rope he needs to hang himself," she surmised aloud.

"Precisely."

And they were both targets.

If there was one thing she had learned, when the CIA wanted a target dead…

…that target usually got dead.

Chapter 12

Olivia couldn't sleep that night.

Jeffrey had finally given up his own battle and started to snore softly. They had talked and he had convinced her to allow him to call his lab tomorrow morning to let the senior scientist know that an emergency had come up. He'd suggested she call her part-time assistant, as well. He was right. She should have thought of that. The last thing she needed right now was someone going to the authorities and reporting them missing.

There was no way either of them was going to be back in L.A. anytime soon.

It was doubtful that, assuming she survived the coming storm, she would be able to return to her life in L.A., period. Jeffrey had a chance, but his odds weren't that much better than hers.

She closed her eyes and fought the need to start grieving her newest life already. She didn't want to think about how upset her patients would be. Sadness welled inside her at the prospect that she probably wouldn't ever see any of them again. She'd grown unexpectedly attached to a couple of them over the past couple of years.

Olivia squeezed her eyes shut and tried to block her thoughts, but that wasn't happening.

She didn't deserve to be betrayed by anyone she'd worked for at the CIA. She'd been extremely dedicated, loyal to a fault. Hamilton, Woods, Echols…the former president himself, not to mention Andrew Page and who knows who else at Interpol.

Why were the men in her life always letting her down?

She turned her head toward the man sleeping next to her. He hadn't actually done anything to hurt her in any way, but then she hadn't let herself get emotionally tangled up with Jeffrey. She liked him a lot. She enjoyed his company. But she wasn't in love with him and if he walked away from the relationship tomorrow, she'd be okay with it. She hadn't been able to let him deep enough inside to have that kind of power.

Landry had done that to her. He'd damaged her to the point that she didn't have the guts to give her heart away again. She couldn't trust on that level.

That kiss earlier tonight zoomed into vivid focus.

Need ached through her. It had been so long since she'd wanted anything that badly. The idea that he could still bring her to that place startled her. It wasn't fair. She didn't want to feel that way about him anymore. Or maybe she did and just didn't want to admit as much.

It would be so much easier to continue hating him.

But that wasn't going to happen, no use pretending.

Jeffrey rolled onto his side and the snoring stopped. Thankfully.

Having him next to her like this felt soothing from a standpoint she recognized was fueled by familiarity and safety and nothing more. He was no threat to her physically or emotionally. Was that fair to him? To allow him to continue to care about her, perhaps even fall in love with her, when she couldn't possibly ever fall in love with him? And all that was assuming he could forgive her for lying to him or that he could get past her former profession.

Where did that leave her?

Alone again.

She turned onto her side, away from him, and stared at the connecting door that separated her room from Landry's. To deny she still cared about him would be a flat-out lie. There were aspects of her emotions over which she had no control. There, far beyond the borders of her reach, she wanted him desperately. Cared for him every bit as much as she had before. They'd been a perfect match, like the final two pieces of a puzzle. His dark, enigmatic traits had drawn her to him in ways she still couldn't explain. Everything about him had completed her, made her whole.

Letting him in on the idea that she still had feelings for him would be another mistake. She might not be able to salvage her heart but at least she could save face.

The sound of Landry moving around in his room drew her attention toward the door once more. Her foolish heart skipped a beat.

Why couldn't she keep hating him?

She rolled onto her back and stared at the ceiling. With the bathroom light on and the door only partially open, the room wasn't completely dark. She never had liked sleeping in the dark.

She almost laughed at herself. A killer who was afraid of the dark.

Was that ridiculous or what?

A soft rap on the connecting door sent her into a sitting position.

Landry rested one foot on her side of the doorway. Judging by the half of him she could see, he appeared to be fully dressed. That was good since she'd seen more than enough of his body already tonight.

"I'm going to take a look around outside," he let her know. "I'm feeling restless."

She threw the covers back and got up, belatedly realizing she'd opted to sleep in her T-shirt only. Damn.

"Any particular reason you can't sleep?" She

wished the tee was a couple of inches longer, but it was too late now. He'd already taken a head-to-toe visual. Her skin felt on fire everywhere his gaze had lingered.

His shoulders moved up and down in a noncommittal gesture. "Feels like something is wrong."

She resisted the urge to say something irreverent like *duh*. "Well, it's not like we have any reason to feel anxious. Someone from our past wants us dead, but that's really no big deal. We should both be sleeping like babies."

Those dark eyebrows drew together in a curious manner. "Funny that you mention *that*. Do you ever wish you'd had a couple?"

Okay, he'd lost her completely. "A couple of what?"

"Babies."

A choked laugh burst out of her before she could close her gaping mouth. "Are you kidding?"

Another of those careless shrugs. "Just wondered. You're at that age when most women claim they can hear their biological clocks ticking."

She was thirty-seven. Big deal. Call her old-fashioned, but she hadn't thought about kids, considering she didn't have a husband.

"I guess you and Jeffrey don't want children."

Oh, now she knew where he was going with this. He wanted to know how serious things were between her and Jeffrey.

She shrugged dramatically, uncaring that the T-shirt had just lifted high enough to give him a sneak peek at her black panties. "I don't know. We're busy people. Maybe sometime. If I live through this, that is."

"Fine." He readied to return to his side of the door. "I'll be back in five."

Well, well. She might not be a mind reader and Landry certainly worked at keeping his thoughts hidden, but she was relatively sure she'd just heard jealousy in his voice.

Then again, the way he'd kissed her pretty much gave away his position on the matter. He still had feelings for her. She definitely wasn't in this fix alone.

Five minutes had come and gone.

Olivia had paced the room about a thousand times in those excruciatingly long seconds.

She was going out there.

Pulling on her jeans, she stuck first one foot then the other into her hiking boots. She snapped her fly then laced her boots and tucked the knife into place just in case. Grabbing her Beretta, she jammed it into her waistband. She silenced her cell phone and slid it into her back pocket. On second thought, she pulled it back out and called Landry's cell. Four rings later it went to voice mail. Where the hell was he?

After shoving her phone back into her pocket, she roused Jeffrey. She'd considered leaving him asleep in the room since this very well could be nothing, but she wasn't willing to take the risk. Protecting him was her responsibility.

"Hey," she murmured. "Something may be wrong. We need to take a walk outside. Get dressed, okay?"

He got up without any fuss and pulled himself together. "What's up?" he asked as they eased into the corridor and headed for the stairwell. No covert-operations agent would ever let himself get trapped in an elevator. To this day Olivia always took the stairs wherever she went.

Inside the stairwell she listened for several seconds to ensure she and Jeffrey were alone.

At 1:00 a.m. she didn't anticipate running into any other guests. Most of the folks who popped into this hotel would be long-distance travelers and sleep would be the only thing on their minds.

When she reached for the railing to start down the stairs, an uneasy feeling swept over her.

She wasn't sure she could trust her instincts enough to assume they had kicked back into gear with any accuracy, but she wasn't imprudent enough to ignore the sensation.

Reaching beneath her T, she wrapped the fingers of her right hand around the butt of her Beretta and withdrew the weapon.

"Is that necessary?" Jeffrey eased up close behind her. "Have they found us?"

"I don't know, but we're not taking any chances. Let's just move down the stairs as quietly as we can."

If she got outside and there was trouble, keeping Jeffrey out of the line of fire wouldn't be an easy thing, considering there wasn't that much cover in the parking lot. About her only option would be the parked vehicles. Better to stash him away, she decided.

They descended one level as quickly and soundlessly as possible. She tucked her weapon back into her waistband and moved into the corridor. She surveyed the rows of closed doors on either side. The vending-machine area was about the only place readily available. Not optimal but it would do.

"This way."

She hurried in that direction. Jeffrey stayed right behind her. Just before she reached the vending-machine area, she passed a door marked Linens. She hesitated, checked the door. Locked. She sized up the situation and decided that wouldn't present a problem.

"Give me your credit card, Jeffrey."

Looking totally confused, he dug out his wallet and produced his platinum Visa. A few jiggles of the knob along with just the right pressure with the credit card and she had the door open.

Jeffrey looked from her to the open door and back. "That's scary."

Olivia smiled. "I know all kinds of tricks like that." She turned on the light and peeked inside. "I want you to hide in here and keep the door locked until I come back for you."

"I'd rather stay with you." Concern cluttered his expression. "I don't want you getting hurt."

This sweet man would be far better off without her.

"Remember, I've got a gun. Just stay in here and don't come out until I come back for you, okay?"

Reluctantly he did as she urged. When the door had closed and she'd heard the lock click, she headed for the stairwell once more.

On ground level, she pressed against the door that would take her outside and listened. She wasn't worried about anyone coming in through this door—it was an exit only. They'd had to walk back to the lobby to reach their room after parking a few hours ago. If trouble had arrived, it would have to come through the lobby to reach her.

A moment's uncertainty trickled through her. Jeffrey should be safe as long as he stayed put. Any scouts that had been sent would be searching rooms, not locked linen closets.

And, bearing in mind what she knew now, this could turn ugly. Ushering Jeffrey outside in the middle of the night only to get shot at wasn't at all appealing.

She steeled herself and slowly pulled the door inward just enough to peek outside. Nothing moved in and around the vehicles she could see beyond the sidewalk at this end of the hotel.

Not wanting to have to go through the lobby in the event she needed to reach the room in a hurry, she bent down and felt around for a large enough nugget of landscaping bark to prevent the door from closing fully once she slipped out.

The night was warm. Humid. And deathly still.

Her pulse skittered, reacting to the faster rhythm of her heart's response to the rising adrenaline.

She edged to the corner of the building and surveyed the front parking area and hotel entrance. Nothing.

Where the hell was Landry?

Moving swiftly, she checked the rear of the building. She almost turned away, assuming the back of the building was as clear as the front. But then she looked again.

The vehicle's engine ran smoothly, quietly. She might not have heard it at all if she hadn't hesitated that extra second. No interior lights, no exterior lights, just an engine running in a beefy black SUV. One very much like the vehicle that had given pursuit at the mall. But she couldn't say for sure it was the same one.

The windows were tinted to the extent that she couldn't see inside.

She needed to be closer.

A lot closer.

Olivia crouched next to the shrubbery line that flanked the building and reviewed her options for getting from point A to point B across the parking lot.

If she stayed close to the building, behind the shrubs that softened the landscape between it and the sidewalk, she would be concealed until she reached the other side of the parking lot. Cars sat in every available space on that end, all the way to the sidewalk.

She could move through the cars until she reached the SUV.

Attempting to maneuver with any speed in a crouched position resulted in a couple of spills, but she made it to the other end of the building. Damn, she was out of practice. A running crouch was not a part of her regular workout these days.

A distance of about ten feet separated the shrub she was currently using as camouflage from the first vehicle she needed to reach. Since she couldn't tell if anyone was in the SUV, she'd just have to risk being seen.

Hunkering as low to the pavement as possible, she scrambled to the first parked vehicle.

She sat very still, trying to hear above her ragged breathing. No door slamming. No running footsteps.

Okay.

Move.

Staying low, she wove through the vehicles. A steadying calm had lapsed over her, allowing her to focus fully on her target.

The SUV sat on the access way between two rows of parked vehicles, facilitating a fast getaway if necessary. The engine was still running. A puddle of water beneath it indicated the air-conditioning was in use.

She had two options here. She could move around the end of the vehicle, stand up and peer through the glass and hope she'd be able to make out anyone inside. Or she could create a distraction.

The distraction won out.

Reaching into her boot, she pulled out the knife. The sharp blade gleamed in the moonlight. This would do the trick.

She reached up and scraped the knife along the cargo door, putting all her weight behind it. The blade screeched along the metal, tearing away a line of paint as it went.

The unmistakable sound of a door opening stopped her dead still. Front driver's side. She eased around to the passenger side of the vehicle, slid the knife back into her boot and waited. She wrapped the fingers of both hands around the butt of the Beretta and prepared to do battle.

"Son of a bitch," rumbled from the rear of the vehicle.

She shot upward, feet landing wide apart, and leveled her aim on the man who stepped around to her side of the vehicle at almost the same time.

"Move and you're dead," she cautioned.

In her peripheral vision she could see that his weapon was in his hand but she kept her eyes on his, didn't let herself get distracted by that detail.

"Put your weapon down, Miss Clark."

She didn't recognize the voice but she did know the face. Same guy she'd told the salesclerk was her boyfriend back at the mall. Only this time he was wearing a dark suit.

"Not a chance. Drop yours and maybe I'll let you live."

"We have your friend."

Dread pricked her. She didn't have to ask who; she knew he meant Jeffrey. Landry wouldn't be caught by these chumps, not alive anyway.

"Prove it." He could be bluffing.

"Linen closet, second floor."

Damn.

"That won't change how I handle this situation." She stared straight into his eyes and hoped like hell he would buy her bluff.

She hadn't killed a man in three years.

Could she do this?

Her heart thumped mercilessly against her chest.

The sound of approaching footsteps behind her had him looking beyond her. His glance past her lasted a fraction of a second, a mere instant, but she reacted.

She fired, hit him just above the knee as she lunged for the ground.

His weapon discharged. The bullet hit the pavement inches from her head.

She rolled. Bumped into the wheel of a nearby car. She scrambled beneath it. Crawled to the other side.

One—no two—sets of running footsteps ricocheted in the night air.

She slid from under the car. Peeked above the vehicle to get a fix on the others.

One man was using Jeffrey as a human shield as he made his way to the SUV. The other was not in sight.

Damn. Damn.

If she tried to take out the guy holding on to Jeffrey…

"You bitch!"

The guy she'd shot was coming after her. The hop-and-drag sound was close. She edged around to the front of the vehicle just as he staggered up behind it. She held her position. Listened intently for him to move closer.

"You should've killed me when you had the chance," he growled.

"You're probably right."

Her breath caught. *Landry*.

She stole a look over the trunk just in time to see Landry bop the guy on the back of the head. He crumpled to the ground and Landry kicked his weapon out of reach.

A bullet glanced off the hood next to Landry. He ducked down. "That was a close one." He peeped above the fender to locate the man dragging Jeffrey toward the SUV.

"Only two?" Olivia wanted to be sure there wasn't more trouble lurking around before she made a move.

"I took care of two others inside." Landry was working his way to the front of the vehicle. "While you were sleeping."

"I wasn't sleeping." She didn't ask…tried not to wonder what he meant when he said he'd taken care of two others. She didn't want to know.

The distant sound of sirens split the night air.

Not good.

Scuffling.

Olivia's heart surged into her throat. She hoped like hell Jeffrey wasn't fighting his captor. One look confirmed her worst fears.

The only man left was attempting to herd Jeffrey into the SUV while keeping a lookout for her and Landry. Jeffrey wasn't cooperating.

She couldn't wait any longer. She had to move.

"Wait, Nessa," Landry hissed.

Not going to happen.

She rushed between the vehicles until she reached the last row next to the SUV.

Holding her breath, she rocketed to a standing position. Leveled her weapon. Took a bead.

And fired.

The shot shattered through the man's right shoulder before he could react, sending a shock wave all the way to his hand. The weapon he held clattered to the pavement. He scrambled to grab it with his left hand but she was over the car's hood and on top of the weapon before he could reach it.

"Get down," she ordered.

Cradling his shoulder, he flattened on the pavement.

With one swift kick she sent his weapon spinning off under the vehicle she'd scrambled across.

"We should tie him up," she told Landry as he jogged up next to her.

"No time. Cops."

He was right. The sirens were very close now.

In one abrupt move, she slammed the butt of her

Beretta into the guy's skull, sending him to la-la land
for a while.

"Thank God you're all right." Jeffrey rushed up
to her, surveyed her from head to toe.

Her relief at seeing that he was unharmed almost
made her sway. "We're all okay."

"Come on!" Landry shouted. "This is not the time."

Seconds later they were in the Land Rover.
Landry executed a U-turn and headed toward the
neighboring parking lot. An IHOP. He didn't take the
usual route, out of the hotel's lot and onto the
highway, to reach the entrance to the IHOP property.
He went straight over the wide median, careful not
to flatten any of the shrubbery.

He drove slowly around to the other side of the
restaurant and backed into a slot.

In the nick of time.

Four police cruisers raced into the hotel's parking
lot. When they'd circled around to the rear of the
building, Landry eased out of his slot and rolled up to
the stop sign where the IHOP lot met the service road.

Cops spilled out of the cruisers and started assess-
ing the threat as well as the condition of the two
downed men.

Landry pulled out onto the service road and
headed toward the ramp to the beltway.

Olivia's chest ached with the breath she'd been
holding, but she couldn't let it go until they were out
of sight of the flashing blue lights.

"They'll get a description of our vehicle," Landry noted.

She knew.

"We'll have to ditch it and find some other means of transportation."

She knew that, too.

"They'll search each room until they determine who isn't accounted for."

Back at the hotel, he meant. "Standard protocol." Again, nothing she didn't know already.

"The Agency's boys may cover for us. Claim jurisdiction and send the locals on their way."

Olivia closed her eyes and let go a shaky breath. She had to know exactly what he'd done back there. An annoying little voice just wouldn't shut up until she knew. "Did you kill anyone?"

The silence that dragged on inside the car was very nearly muffled by the roar of blood in her ears.

"No."

Profound relief swamped her.

"But I would have if necessary. Do you have a problem with that?"

How could she say yes? Hysterical laughter gurgled up into her throat at the same time that tears burned at the backs of her eyes.

She'd killed for a living. Had been the best of the best. And now the mere idea of taking a life ripped her apart inside. As proudly as she had served her country, that one mistake—that one killing of a man who shouldn't have been a target—had ruined her. She couldn't do it anymore.

Pull it together, she ordered. This was no time to crack. She took a breath and gave him the only answer she could, "I don't know."

That was where the conversation ended.

Landry drove. He took side streets. He made a million turns.

She sat there in the dark, numb and exhausted.

Jeffrey did the same.

She could only imagine how he felt just now.

They needed another car.

Everything they'd had with them, including the money, was back in that hotel room.

She told herself she'd been in worse situations.

It was true.

But it gave her no comfort.

Olivia couldn't be sure how much time had passed when Landry at last stopped the car.

He parked inside an out-of-business car wash and turned around to face her. Without the aid of the dash lights, she couldn't see his expression or hope to assess his mood in the consuming darkness.

"There's a car on the street about a block from here. I'm going to check it out. If it's functional, I'll come back for you. If it's not, I'll keep looking until I find something that is. Stay here. I'll call you if I run into any trouble."

He opened the driver's-side door but no light

came on inside the vehicle, providing some amount of relief. He'd had the foresight to turn the switch to the off position before opening the door. Any light, at this time of night, in this run-down neighborhood would attract attention. Especially in view of the fact that they were parked in a closed-for-business car wash. They didn't need any attention.

Still, she would have liked to see Landry's face... to get some idea of what he was thinking.

That was a lie. She could never read him. She simply wanted to see him...just in case.

Before he closed the door she blurted, "Be careful."

She hadn't meant to let that slip out. Dammit.

"I will be back, Nessa. You have my word."

The door closed with a thud.

She sat there. Didn't turn around to try and see him moving through the night. She didn't do anything.

Except the most unlikely act for a former assassin.

She prayed.

Chapter 13

The sound of a running engine pulled Olivia's attention toward the street.

Her Beretta palmed, she moved cautiously to the entrance of the dilapidated car wash and surveyed the street, left then right.

She'd left Jeffrey in the SUV and had taken a position where she could keep an eye open for the unexpected. She didn't need any more surprises tonight.

Now that the mega blast of adrenaline from all the excitement at the hotel had dissipated for the most part, she'd had time to think. How had those men found them at the hotel?

The bigger question was, why weren't they dead already?

A car approached from the right. Black or dark blue. Headlights were off.

Olivia slipped back into the shadow of the building and waited for the vehicle to come closer.

If any of the streetlights in this neighborhood still worked, she might be able to make out the number of occupants before they were on top of her. But vandals had put them out of commission, and the city had apparently opted not to keep up the maintenance.

She controlled her respiration, forced her heart to slow its reaction to the new trickle of adrenaline. At one time she'd been particularly good at this discipline.

A head leaned out the driver's-side window.

Landry.

She relaxed. He'd kept the headlights off so as not to attract any unnecessary attention from the houses flanking the narrow street.

For the first time since this game began, she admitted to herself that she was glad he was here. As much as she hated to admit it, she'd never been any good at hot-wiring a vehicle. And they needed a way out of here.

As he made the turn into the car-wash lot, she hustled over to the SUV to get Jeffrey.

"Let's go. We have new transportation."

He got out slowly. Didn't speak.

"Jeffrey." She touched his shoulder. "Are you okay?"

He nodded. "I'm fine."

The pressure of regret pressing against her chest made taking a deep breath difficult. He wasn't fine.

"I'm really sorry about all of this." There was more she wanted to say but right now they had to go.

He turned his face to her. Even in the near-total darkness she could see the devastation, or maybe she sensed it more than she actually saw it. "Those men were going to kill you."

Probably. Olivia gathered her determination and reached for him. "We'll be okay." She closed her fingers around his hand. For a couple of seconds his hand remained limp, unresponsive, and then he curled his fingers around hers and nodded.

Uneasiness slid through her when she turned to head toward the waiting car and found Landry waiting at the entrance to the car wash.

"There something we need to do before we go any farther."

Her guard went up. She didn't need ESP to know where this was going. He'd wondered how those men found them the same as she had. The difference was, he'd reached a conclusion she refused to even consider.

"You don't have any proof," she countered before he could toss the first accusation.

"What happened back at the hotel is proof enough. Unless you're going to tell me that you tipped them off." He hadn't drawn his weapon, but his stance was battle ready. Landry wouldn't be backing off on this one.

As much as she hated to admit it, he was right. She could pretend, but she knew.

If anyone was going to do this, it would be her. She turned to Jeffrey, who waited next to her. "Jeffrey, so you understand the situation. We have reason to believe that those guys back at the hotel found us because of a mistake one of us may have made."

"A mistake?"

The confusion in his tone made her feel like a heel. But he was the logical candidate.

"One of us may unknowingly be leading them right to our position."

He looked past her to Landry, then swung his attention back to her. "Are you suggesting me?" He released her hand and flared his fingers, palms up. "I don't even know these people. How could I be passing along information?"

That guilt nagged at her again. "I'm sorry. I'm certain nothing you did was intentional, but we have to know for sure. We can't risk them catching up with us again. We might not be so lucky next time."

He walked past her, came to a halt right in front of Landry and held out his arms, offering access. "Check me out. I have nothing to hide."

Olivia sighed, heading over to stand next to him. "Jeffrey, this isn't personal. The enemy could have found an opportunity to plant some sort of bug before any of this started." There were all sorts of new technologies. Stuff she hadn't even heard of.

He grabbed his cell from his pocket and thrust it at the other man. "View my recent calls."

Landry took the BlackBerry, a specialized cell phone with options like Internet access, walked over to the SUV and used the interior light to inspect the high-tech communications device.

Olivia was pretty sure he wouldn't find anything in Jeffrey's phone. She checked all their communications devices regularly. She put her hand on his arm. He moved away from her touch. That too-familiar regret pricked her. "Someone may be using you, Jeffrey. It isn't your fault. But we have to protect ourselves."

That he refused to talk to her only made her feel worse. As much as she wished this step wasn't necessary, she couldn't deny the absolute urgency of what Landry was doing that very minute.

The crack of plastic slamming onto concrete had her wheeling around to see what Landry was up to. He'd tossed Jeffrey's cell phone onto the ground and now proceeded to shatter it with the heel of his boot.

Jeffrey released a heavy breath but kept whatever he thought to himself.

Landry strode back to where she and Jeffrey waited.

"There was a tracking device in his phone?"

She found that difficult to believe, since she'd inspected Jeffrey's as well as her own phone just a few days ago. Some microfiber job on his clothes possibly, but this, impossible.

"Nothing so simple." Landry rubbed the back of

his neck. "I've only seen this technology used once. It's integrated with the hardware so seamlessly it's almost impossible to spot, but it was there. There could be others in his clothes." He settled his attention on her. "Or your own. How often did you perform a scan of your home?"

She hadn't…at least nothing more than a visual after that first year.

Her hesitation was answer enough.

"I should have a look at your phone, as well."

She wanted to be outraged, but he was right. Without a word, she handed the phone to him.

He walked back to the SUV and did what he had to do.

When he returned, he handed the undamaged phone back to her. "Yours is clean. My guess is they assumed you would examine it regularly and didn't want to risk you'd recognize whatever technology they used."

But she probably wouldn't have…just like she hadn't with Jeffrey's. She'd slipped into some level of complacency. Tried to be normal….

"What now?" She battled the emotions whirling inside her, throwing her off balance.

"We'll drive until we locate an all-night superstore, then we'll get new clothes for the two of you. Just in case."

She nodded. "No point taking any unnecessary risks."

Jeffrey took the backseat in the old pimped-up Caddy. He said nothing to Olivia as he settled there.

She got into the front passenger seat and buckled up.

Landry didn't look at her as he dropped behind the wheel. He backed up then pulled out onto the street and drove through the neighborhood without the aid of headlights.

The silence quickly became suffocating. But what was there to say? She stuck by her belief in Hamilton. He'd never let her down before…why would he do that now? Things changed, she understood that, but if he'd wanted her taken down he really would have done so the night she showed up alone at his weekend home, whether he also wanted Landry or not.

Twenty minutes later they were on the interstate again, traveling back toward the Arlington area. A quick stop at a superstore and she and Jeffrey were decked out in new duds, shoes included. Going to that extreme might have been unnecessary, but why take any chances?

Olivia had used the lack of conversation in the car as an opportunity to mull over all that had happened. She'd arrived at a conclusion as to what her next move should be.

With that in mind, she announced, "I want to talk to Hamilton again."

That Landry remained focused completely on the long stretch of highway in front of them and refused to even glance her way sent up warning flags.

He didn't agree.

She didn't care. Nothing he said could convince

her not to go to the one man she'd trusted three years ago.

"We both know Hamilton is in the game. You've already confronted him at his weekend home," Landry offered. "Don't you find it odd that he hasn't tried to contact you since your meeting with Director Woods?"

Olivia considered that her old Sheara number was forwarded to her current cell number. Hamilton could contact her if he so chose, she imagined. But the idea that he might avoid contact in case he was being watched carried just as much weight as any other.

Another aspect of the events that had occurred over the past forty-eight hours abruptly cleared for her. "I don't think they're trying to kill us."

"It does appear as if they've sent their most inept men after us," Landry allowed, following her train of thought. "Avoiding capture has been a little easier than it should have been."

Damn straight it had been. As rusty as she was, she sure couldn't claim skill. "But what do they want?"

"To determine just what we know. To make sure we haven't told anyone."

Olivia chewed on her lower lip. "That would mean torture. Lots of it."

The idea of how this conversation sounded had her looking back to check on Jeffrey. He stared out the window, seemingly oblivious to the conversation in the front seat, but she knew better.

"They'll use us against each other."

She shifted her attention back to Landry, dread congealing in her gut.

"They will."

"Bottom line, we appear to have ahead of us a command performance with whoever is in charge," Landry suggested.

Something else to look forward to. "A debrief."

A crash catch-up course on ways to inflict pain sounded less than appealing. But they couldn't stop now. They had to finish this…or they'd both be running for the rest of their lives.

"If Hamilton isn't next on our agenda, then who?" She wanted to talk to him again, but that might serve no other purpose than to get them caught. That was exactly what would be expected of her. She'd already proven that once when Landry had caught her there. Being predictable equated to being stupid.

"Echols."

"What about Page?" That Landry continued to bypass the names from his side of the covert-operations world annoyed her probably more than it should have.

"Page is the one who warned me that trouble was headed our way, remember? He also helped me find you."

He had mentioned that. But did that prove anything?

"You haven't considered that his warning could have been the catalyst for this operation?"

Everyone who knew she was alive and who had been involved in that op three years ago was a suspect. She and Landry had agreed on that already. There was no rational reason for him to see it any other way. His people were just as susceptible to slipping into the dark side as hers.

Page had saved his life. So what? Hamilton had, too. Page had warned him. Big deal. Hamilton had promised to help her. Echols and the former president had everything to lose. No one was exempt. That he'd managed to position himself so close to the current president was a rare phenomenon. One he would likely want to protect.

"I know Page. He isn't the one."

"But you listed him in your initial lineup of suspects."

"Only because I knew you would notice if I didn't." He glanced at her for the first time since the conversation had started. "And I was right."

No matter how she looked at it, some aspects still didn't add up. Both Hamilton and Page had the resources to take them down with far less effort and drama than they'd experienced so far. Maybe bringing them in alive was priority as they'd discussed moments ago.

It was crazy but here she was, a former CIA agent, Landry a former Interpol agent, and even working together they were no closer to the truth now than they had been forty-eight hours ago.

She collapsed more deeply into her seat and considered the best way to proceed. Maybe Landry was right and Echols should be next on their agenda, but there were other concerns that needed to be addressed.

Like Jeffrey.

She couldn't continue to expose him to this level of danger. If he were with them when they were caught he would be terminated, as well. She couldn't let that happen. Running for the rest of their lives wasn't feasible. Not like this.

Alternate plans had to be made.

"I need a hotel and a couple of hours before we do anything else," she said.

"A couple hours of sleep would be good for all of us."

Sleep wasn't what she had on her mind but Landry didn't need to know that.

This was personal.

And it wouldn't wait any longer.

The hotel was a step above the last one. But that wasn't important.

Landry had only gotten one room. He'd used another of his many aliases and accompanying credit cards. She didn't bother asking which one. It wouldn't matter.

Jeffrey sat down on the edge of the bed. He hadn't asked any questions or offered any comments since they left the out-of-business car wash.

Olivia turned to Landry. "I need some time with Jeffrey. Can you take a walk?"

This was a fairly exclusive part of town and it was

approaching 5:00 a.m. Surely there was a coffee shop or diner nearby that opened by five.

He didn't look happy but he didn't argue. "I'll be back in an hour. We'll need to get moving soon."

"Whatever."

When Landry had gone, Olivia sat down on the bed next to Jeffrey. Sleep would have to wait. "We should talk about this."

He drew in a deep breath and let it out in one long whoosh. "Actually I keep hoping I'll wake up and discover this has all been one really long nightmare."

She had to smile. "I'm truly sorry for all of this, Jeffrey." She'd said it so many times she hoped it still sounded genuine.

He lifted one shoulder and let it fall. "I suppose I should be thankful."

She frowned, couldn't see how he would feel grateful in any capacity.

"I'm certain I would never have been dragged about, almost kidnapped and used as a walking, talking tracking device if not for my relationship with you."

She laughed. Couldn't help herself. The sound was strained but it was better than crying.

He looked at her and then he laughed, too.

Several minutes elapsed before they'd regained their composure.

"You are an exceptional man, Jeffrey." That same old regret and maybe a little sadness enveloped her.

He took her hand in his and managed a damn

decent smile. "It's you who is exceptional, Olivia. In all my life I've never met a woman so extraordinary."

Why couldn't she be in love with this man? It would be so easy…so safe.

"I don't deserve that compliment." Guilt plagued her. She'd let Jeffrey care about her and she hadn't been able to reciprocate to the same extent.

"Yes, you do." He stared at their entwined hands. "But I know whatever we had is over. Maybe it never really was."

"I do care about you, Jeffrey." She needed him to know that.

He laughed softly. "I know you do. But I also know that you love *him*."

Her breath trapped in her throat and it took every ounce of strength she had not to let the tears crowding against her lashes fall. "I tried not to. I told myself for three years that I hated him. That if given the chance, I'd kill him."

Jeffrey cleared his throat and pressed his free hand to his chest. "I still have trouble with that part. I just can't see you as an assassin. I know how much you care for your patients. It just doesn't fit the Olivia I know."

She searched those brown eyes for pain or anger and found nothing but resignation and affection. "I'm not that person anymore. Maybe I never was. Sheara was a persona I slipped into in order to be what the CIA needed me to be. To serve my country. At the time I was convinced it was the right thing to do. I guess that's why I took the easy way out when the opportunity arose."

A frown marred his smooth brow. "I don't understand what you mean."

She hadn't admitted this to anyone. "I didn't try to fight what happened three years ago. I could have done something. Demanded an inquiry. Stood up for myself. I probably wouldn't have won, might even have ended up dead, but I could have tried. But vanishing was the route I took. The easy way out. Maybe I'd been looking for an excuse to become someone else. I don't know."

Jeffrey's smile was understanding. "Sounds as if Dr. Mills has been doing some self-analyzing."

"Maybe. I just know that I can't go back. Whatever happens in the next twenty-four hours, I have to get through it without taking a life. I don't think I can do that again."

Jeffrey took her by the shoulders and made her look directly into his eyes. "Olivia, you know how I feel about guns in general. I'm antiwar, anti…well, lots of things. But I want you to swear to me that you will do whatever necessary to survive this."

He was just too damn sweet. She almost lost the battle with the tears. "Jeffrey, I—"

"I mean it," he said sternly. "You do whatever you have to do to survive."

His words shored up her waning determination.

"I will," she relented when his gaze pressed her for an answer.

"Good." He let go of her and seemed uncertain

what to do with his hands until he'd dropped them to his lap.

"I don't know how this will turn out," she ventured. This next part was crucial. It was abundantly clear that the real threat had never been to him. He'd been a mere pawn. Keeping him in the line of fire any longer was unconscionable. "But I don't want you at risk anymore."

"I'm fine, really. I'll be okay."

She shook her head. "I can't risk your exposure to what may happen next."

"Olivia—"

"Jeffrey—" she cut off his argument "—you could become a liability. Any distraction could get me killed."

That appeared to give him pause. "I hadn't thought of that."

"I'd like you to stay here. Landry will ensure the room is covered for however long it takes."

"I have money," he countered.

"I don't want you to do anything that will draw attention to you. Don't use a credit card or ATM card. Nothing. Just stay here in the room. Use all the room service you want. Watch television. Movies. Just don't leave the room."

"For how long?"

She knew he was thinking of his work again.

"This will all be over soon. I'll call you and let you know it's safe to return to L.A."

His eyes searched hers. "You'll call?"

As long as she was alive she would. She supposed that was what he was getting at.

"If you don't hear from me in the next seven days, I want you to withdraw all your liquid assets as discreetly as possible. As well as mine." She grabbed the pad and pen on the bedside table and jotted down her account numbers and associated pins. She fixed her gaze on his so there would be no misunderstanding as regards her intent. "Disappear. Don't go back to L.A. unless I tell you it's safe to. Between the two of us we have sufficient money for you to build a new life somewhere else. New name. The whole works."

"No." He shook his head adamantly. "I'll wait for your call."

She fisted her fingers in his shirtfront and forced him to look at her. "I don't know if I'll survive, Jeffrey. I hope I do, but I can't make that promise. But you can. I need you to promise me that you'll do exactly as I say."

Emotion glittered in his eyes and it was all Olivia could do to restrain her own. This was so unfair to him. He hadn't asked for any of this…hadn't done anything to deserve it.

"All right. Whatever you say. I'll wait one week. If I don't hear from you I'll take…the money and move to…" His mouth worked with uncertainty but no words came out.

"Don't tell me where you'll go." She thought of all those torture techniques she'd taken extensive training in order to endure. She'd experienced her share in the past. Anything she knew could become fair game. No matter how strong a person, everyone had their weakness. The right technician with just the right technique could find it.

Jeffrey nodded. "So, I guess this is goodbye."

Her chest felt so tight she couldn't draw in a deep enough breath. Admittedly she wasn't in love with him, but she did care very much about him. "I guess so."

He got to his feet. "Well, I…" He glanced around the room. "I should get some sleep."

Olivia rose, the weight of yet another change in her life feeling heavier than ever. But it was the right thing to do. She went on tiptoe and kissed his jaw. "I won't ever forget you, Jeffrey."

He stared down at her, his feelings of affection abundantly clear. "Nor I you."

For three beats she battled the impulse to kiss him, really kiss him. But that would be a mistake. Would only hurt both of them when she walked out that door. Instead, she smiled and for one sentimental moment she let herself recall the good times they'd had together.

The moment passed and she mentally geared up for what had to come next.

"I should call Landry and let him know I'm ready to go."

She reached into her jeans pocket for her cell but Jeffrey stopped her with a hand on her arm.

"Just one more thing."

She tried to read the abrupt change in his expression, but it was a look totally uncharacteristic for the man with whom she'd shared so very much. "Yes?"

"Tell Landry that if he hurts you again I will hunt him down and kick his ass."

Chapter 14

Olivia considered the home of Paul Echols. Nine-teenth century, in the famed historic section of George-town, minutes from his upwardly mobile career in D.C. He owned two Mercedes and had one child in the most prestigious private school in the area. His wife was the quintessential socialite, ensuring the Echols name was on elegantly embossed invitations originat-ing from the addresses of the politically prominent.

The neighborhood was the reason they'd had to take the time to borrow new transportation. The other vehicle would have stood out on this street.

Before long, dawn would be stretching its pink and purple fingers across the sky. Olivia, for one, would be thankful for the coming light. Sitting here for more than an hour, in the dark, with Landry was beginning to get to her in ways that could only lead to trouble.

It hadn't been so bad before, when Jeffrey was with them. But now, with only the two of them, the tension had started to thicken in the air. Made breathing near impossible.

She had intended to get a couple of hours' sleep before launching into this morning's critical surveillance, but neither she nor Landry had been able to wait.

In fact, she'd wanted to make *the* call a full sixty minutes ago, but Landry had insisted they needed to watch for a while first. Determine if Echols appeared to be going about life as usual.

Olivia really didn't know the man except by sight. She, of course, understood the position he'd held in the previous White House administration, but there had been no reason for her to have been acquainted with him.

Part of his job as a special adviser to the president would have been to keep him abreast of the ramifications of such sensitive operations as the one Olivia had carried out three years ago. Echols was the moderator. The neutral voice in such sensitive matters.

"We should make the call," she said again, frustrated with the waiting. Going crazy breathing the air permeated with the subtle scent that was uniquely Holt Landry. Her entire body tingled with a simmering anticipation that would be assuaged by only one thing.

And that wasn't going to happen.

"We should be patient," Landry countered, his deep, refined voice husky from lack of sleep or maybe his own mounting tension.

The car was compact, too cramped for her liking. With no console between the driver's seat and the one she occupied, they sat almost elbow to elbow.

"Finish your coffee."

The extra-large white cup sat on the dash, still half full of the now-cold mega-strong brew they'd picked up at a drive-through before arriving in Echols's swanky neighborhood.

"Right, and then I'll be making a run for the shrubbery." She surveyed the meticulously landscaped lawns along the street, each lit with just the right ambient lighting. Once upon a time she'd sat through all-night surveillances without needing a nature break, but she'd grown far too soft for that now.

The silence that followed had her mind wandering into dangerous territory again.

Landry hadn't really changed that much. The image of his muscular torso popped into her head. He'd stayed in shape, which wasn't surprising since he'd been very athletic when she knew him…before.

For the first time since he'd plowed back into her life, she wondered about the women he'd been with since they parted ways. She mentally rolled her eyes and wanted to kick herself for even thinking about it.

She'd had her share of one-night stands. Had lived

with Jeffrey for six months, and dated him for three months before that. She certainly couldn't expect that Landry had remained celibate. That would be ludicrous, considering the voracious sexual appetite she recalled quite vividly.

Warmth stirred deep inside her as images from the past filtered through her mind before she could stop them. Okay, so maybe this wasn't a good distraction to pass the time. They were on surveillance duty. Focus, Olivia.

"I assume you let Jeffrey down easy."

Landry's statement yanked her from the thoughts she shouldn't be thinking. "I beg your pardon?" The conversation between her and Jeffrey was none of his business.

"You and Jeffrey. The relationship. It's over?"

Landry turned his face in her direction. The meager light offered by the coming dawn allowed her to make out the firm set of his jaw. She couldn't read his eyes, too dark. The one thing she could sense above all else was the way his nearness drew her.

"What makes you think it's over?" Dumb, Olivia.

He turned his attention forward again. "I just assumed you'd realized your mistake."

A burst of disbelief blew past her lips in the form of a choked laugh. "My *mistake?* You've got some nerve, Landry." She gripped the door's armrest tightly to hold on to her anger. "The only mistake I've ever made is getting mixed up with you."

Why the hell were they even having this conversation now? Because it was the safest way? This was the way it had always been. They had both used the danger…the extreme nature of their professions to cushion the personal relationship. She recognized that now for what it was, a way to maintain distance. And she was every bit as guilty as he was.

For about ten seconds she thought he wasn't going to respond. What did it matter? The next few hours would determine if they survived or not. What was the point of discussing anything until they knew if tomorrow would come?

"I don't believe you."

Her eyes widened with disbelief. Was he trying to start an argument? Well, by God, she wasn't taking the bait.

"Believe what you want." She never took her gaze off the Echols's home.

His silence sent satisfaction, if not victory, roaring through her. The very idea that he would make a statement like that. Cocky bastard.

"When you're ready to admit you're in denial we'll talk."

She glared at him. "I am not in denial," she returned calmly, too calmly.

He turned that dark head and looked her straight in the eye. "I kissed you, remember? I know I wasn't the only one who wanted more. You still have feelings for me."

She crossed her arms over her chest and refocused her gaze on the Echols's house. Though there wasn't much light, she wasn't about to risk him seeing the truth in her eyes. "Get a grip, Landry. Don't confuse a physical need with an emotional attachment. Whatever you think you felt when you kissed me was about sex, nothing more."

He reached over and grabbed her hand, his knuckles brushing the underside of her breast, sending a fierce longing through her. "Then you won't mind if I hold your hand for a bit."

Fine, let him push the issue. He always had to prove his point. "You're crazy."

"Maybe."

Hauling her full attention to the Echols's home once more, she hoped he'd make a move, any move—soon. This Monday morning Echols appeared to be in no hurry to get out and about. It was going on seven. Surely it wouldn't be that much longer. She really hoped he didn't plan to have a leisurely breakfast with his family. She wanted *this* over.

The feel of Landry's thumb making suggestive little circles in her palm tugged at her. She kept her hand limp, wouldn't give him the satisfaction of knowing how even that small movement affected her.

"There hasn't been a night in the past three years that I haven't lain in bed and thought about you. Missed you."

Olivia tugged to free her hand from his but he held

on, wouldn't let go. Dammit. "Can we focus here, Landry?"

"This might be the only time we have together."

Jeez, now he was playing dirty. She'd just have to use another tactic. Anything to keep him from guessing her true feelings and to keep this conversation out of even more dangerous territory.

"A guilty conscience will do that, you know. Haunt you."

That persistent thumb stopped, but he didn't let go.

"That was part of it," he confessed.

She looked at him then. Stared hard through the semidarkness. If his voice hadn't sounded so raw…so wounded, she might have been able to pretend his attention was just a game…a way to pass the time and distract her from the call she wanted to make.

But she couldn't pretend. She knew what she'd heard.

"You knew where I was." That she'd let the hurt and vulnerability come out in that statement made her want to snatch back the words. But it was true. There was no denying how she felt on that score.

"You were safe. I didn't want to disrupt the careful world you'd built. I couldn't take that risk, Nessa. Olivia," he amended. "You'd been through enough. As much as I wanted to be with you, I wanted you safe even more."

Okay. Enough. She was not going there right now. "Whatever you say."

He exhaled a heavy breath. She refused to shift her attention from their target again even if her curiosity was killing her to analyze his expression.

"I don't know what to say to convince you except that, even when I watched you allow Jeffrey into your life, I couldn't be with anyone else."

Disbelief, confusion and so many other emotions that she couldn't separate one from the other rushed over her. She couldn't quantify the revelation. Three years and no one…he'd stayed faithful to her? How was she supposed to process that information?

"I can't talk about this right now." It was too much to expect.

All she'd learned in the study of the human psyche escaped her at the moment. She couldn't comprehend the scope of his admission. Completely unexpected. Had she really meant that much to him? There was a time when she'd thought so. She wrestled her thoughts back to the matter at hand, watching for a reaction from Echols.

For several moments Landry said nothing more. She spent some of that time stealing glimpses of his profile as night's shadows slowly gave way to gray light. Those lean, chiseled angles that had once driven her crazy with desire made her want to reach out and touch him just to make sure he was real. He was here. He'd come to help her…to protect her. He'd been watching her all this time. Calling just to hear the sound of her voice.

"You were the one, Nessa," he said softly, his

gaze still dead ahead. "I didn't expect to have to go on with my life without you."

All the guilt she had hoped he'd felt for the past three years suddenly dumped on her shoulders.

"The truth is," she anted up, "I did what I had to do in an effort to erase the memory of you." There. She'd said it.

She battled with the emotions twisting inside. Why the hell had she let this conversation slip into this territory?

"We should…" He reached out and gripped the steering wheel, maybe for something to do with his hands instead of touching her. "I don't know…" He glanced at her before shifting his gaze back to the target. "Maybe take a look at *us* again…if we survive."

She had to touch him. A simple caress of his lean, beard-shadowed jaw. It felt good to touch him that way. His eyes closed as if he too reveled in the sensation.

How could she have pretended that she hated him for a minute, much less three years? She'd been lying to herself. Trying to go on. Pretending the past was over…didn't matter.

"I agree." She managed a shaky smile. "And so you know, Jeffrey and I parted as friends. For me, that's really all it ever was."

When she would have drawn her hand away, he took it, drew it to his lips and brushed a kiss across her knuckles.

She stared into those blue eyes and for the first time in three years she felt herself slipping away, getting lost the way she did when they first met…so long ago. He'd had that power over her then…he had it now.

Lights came on in the downstairs portion of the Echols's house, snapping their collective attention to their mission.

Dangerous, Olivia, she chastised. Don't let yourself get that distracted again. If they wanted to survive, she'd sure as hell have to do better than this.

"Well, well," Landry said, "our boy is up and at 'em."

"I'm making that call now."

Landry watched the house while she entered the series of numbers that would connect her to Echols's home number as well as block her number from showing up on his caller ID. Of course, a guy like him could easily have her call tracked down, but her effort would buy them some time.

Echols answered on the second ring.

"Mr. Echols, this is the past calling with a warning. Ancient history is about to come back to haunt you."

She and Landry exchanged a look. The tension inside the vehicle escalated, the source wholly different now.

"Who is this?" Echols demanded.

She smiled at his impatience. He was far too important to bother with a nuisance like her.

"Your worst nightmare, Mr. Echols. This is Vanessa Clark, the CIA agent your administration ordered to eliminate a high-profile Middle Eastern target. Sound familiar?"

"Miss Clark, I'm certain I have no idea what you're suggesting."

She laughed drily. "Then I would suggest that you ask your good friend Director Woods or his deputy. Today's the day, Mr. Echols. I want my life back. I'm coming for it."

Olivia ended the call.

Landry gifted her with one of his particularly charming smiles. "Very good, Agent Clark. You sounded just like the girl I used to know."

Problem was, she wasn't that girl anymore.

Fifteen minutes later the front door opened and Mr. Paul Echols hustled down to the cobblestone drive in front of his house, loaded into the black Mercedes and pulled out onto the street.

"Here we go."

Landry waited an adequate amount of time before easing away from the curb and following the same route Echols had taken.

At 7:00 a.m. traffic was still fairly light. Olivia remembered clearly that by half past seven the situation would be vastly different.

Echols was no fool. He took a number of unnecessary turns to ensure he wasn't tailed. He could take all the turns and evasive maneuvers he wanted. Olivia wasn't worried. Like her, Landry was a master at sticking to a target.

At 7:33 he stopped at a park that was well off the beaten path. One she didn't readily recognize. Not that she'd spent that much time visiting the local parks. She hadn't. She'd been too focused on her career to take time for anything so domestic.

Landry's question about whether she'd thought about having babies popped into her head. The memory startled her all over again. Why would he ask that? *You were the one, Nessa.*

She banished the thoughts. She couldn't think about that right now. It was too overwhelming. Too unexpected. All this time she'd thought she knew how it was. He hadn't cared. He'd walked away. Could she have been this wrong?

Stop it. Focus. Olivia surveyed what she could see of the park. Their survival depended upon her keeping herself together right now. She couldn't let anything else interfere.

At this hour the park was deserted. Echols didn't get out of the car. He was waiting for someone.

Anticipation pumped harder through her veins.

Olivia couldn't wait to identify whoever had betrayed both her and Landry. He would pay. She told herself that over and over. The anger helped her stay focused.

Most likely someone from the very agency to which she'd entrusted her life, for whom she'd carried out dozens of missions. How could none of that matter?

No make-believe this go-round.

Landry had parked their borrowed car in the trees near the entrance of the park. They were well hidden yet their target, in the parking area near the water below their position, was in plain sight. Moving closer would not be necessary until whoever Echols waited for arrived.

Her mind tried to drift back to her and Landry's earlier conversation. She brutally lugged it back to the business at hand. Not right now. Again she reminded herself that the next hour or so was far too important to their survival for her to let anything distract her.

But the silence was driving her out of her mind.

"You never did tell me who lent you the house." She'd been curious about that. He hadn't mentioned it again. That seemed like a safe enough topic.

His eyes met hers briefly, but neither of them wanted to risk missing anything going on below. "The house belongs to Andrew. He bought it as a birthday present for his wife."

She should have suspected as much.

"The Land Rover was his, as well?"

"No. That was mine."

Was being the operative word. The SUV was likely in about a hundred pieces now at some chop shop, since they'd had to abandon it on the less desirable side of town.

"You might be able to buy it back when it hits the black market." A smile spread across her lips at his testy glare.

Then there was the problem that the car they were in was stolen. She hoped the owner slept in. Having the vehicle reported stolen this morning could cramp their plans.

More of that awkward silence.

She shifted in her seat, unable to just sit there. Between the anticipation of what would happen next with Echols and being shut up in this small car so long with Landry, she couldn't sit still.

She needed air. "I'm getting out."

Her cell phone vibrated. A new kind of tension coiled inside her. "It's my phone." She reached into the back pocket of her jeans and tugged it out. The flashing icon on the display indicated it was a forwarded call.

A call for Sheara.

"It's Hamilton." She didn't need to wonder. No one else could possibly have that number.

Landry looked from her to the car parked down by the water and back. "Be very careful what you say."

She nodded then opened the phone. "I've been waiting for your call."

"Good God Almighty," Hamilton gasped. "I've been trying for twenty-four hours to reach you."

She wanted to believe him. He sounded sincere. "You had the number," she countered.

"No," he argued, "I didn't. I sank your file three years ago, remember? That included all the information I had on your code name. I had a hell of a time tracking down this number in some of my old personal files."

"Do you have useful information for me?"

"Vanessa, there are a lot of things I can't explain right now, but I need you to trust me."

She considered her response carefully. "That's asking a lot."

"No matter what happens," he reiterated, "remember that you can trust me. And for God's sake, whatever you do, keep your head down."

Landry tapped his watch. She couldn't stay on any longer.

"Sorry, Hamilton, but I have to go now. I have my own plans." She closed the phone, severing the connection.

"We have company."

Landry was right. Another vehicle had entered the park. A limousine. That most likely meant a high-level official. She did not want it to be Hamilton. And she really didn't want it to be Woods.

Her heart bumped into double time.

"We need to move closer." She was already opening her door when she made the suggestion.

Landry put a hand on her arm. "No sudden moves. Lay low and listen. This is reconnaissance only. We're not prepared to make an aggressive move. Understood?"

"Understood."

Emerging from the vehicle with an efficiency of movement and little or no sound, she and Landry stole through the thicket of trees surrounding the park until they reached a position within hearing range of their targets.

Echols had exited his Mercedes and now waited for his contact to do the same.

The driver of the limo didn't get out. The rear door on the side facing away from their position opened.

Olivia held her breath.

Didn't want to miss a word.

Maybe if her instincts had been as sharp as they once were...if she hadn't let herself go soft for the past three years...then just maybe she would have heard the enemy's approach from the rear.

But she didn't.

Landry, however, did. But his attempt to protect her from the threat cost him any advantage he would have had.

"Drop your weapons."

Her hands held out in the open, she turned slowly to face the man who'd issued the order.

"I said, drop your weapons," he repeated.

She recognized him immediately as one of the four who'd shown up at the hotel the night before. Definitely not one of the ones she'd shot.

That was probably a good thing, otherwise she might be even sorrier than she already was. He'd brought along two of his friends. She supposed the party would begin now.

The guy with his muzzle boring into Landry's skull barked, "You heard him. Drop your weapon."

No agent ever wanted to give up his gun, but there were times when the choice was not your own.

Olivia knew Landry wouldn't go first. Men and their damn pride. He would die before he'd throw down his weapon.

She, on the other hand, had a plan B.

She reached for her Beretta—

"Left hand," her captor cautioned. "Slow and easy."

"Whatever." She slowly reached, with her left hand, beneath her shirt and pulled the weapon from her waistband. She crouched with the same caution and placed it on the ground then kicked it a few feet away. She knew the drill. No need to make this part difficult.

Landry sent a sidelong glance in her direction, which garnered him a kick in the gut.

He doubled over and the jerk who had a bead on him snagged his Glock, checked it out before tossing it onto the ground next to Olivia's weapon.

"Check for backup pieces," the third man, the one who appeared to be in charge, ordered as he moved closer.

This one looked ready to snap Olivia's neck just for the fun of it. Maybe one of the guys she'd shot was his brother or something. Whatever the case, he looked pissed.

Landry's new friend was busily patting him down already, moving quickly and efficiently. No man wanted to linger when feeling up another dude so intimately.

On the other hand, her guy took his time.

She let him, didn't resist. Maybe if he got a little too distracted he wouldn't notice the knife tucked into her shoe.

The .32 Jeffrey had lost landed on the ground next to the Beretta and the Glock. She flashed Landry an annoyed look, and he shrugged. Evidently Jeffrey had dropped it in the SUV she'd rented and Landry had found it.

Her new friend had crouched in front of her. She spread her legs wider to facilitate his efforts. The wicked gleam in his eyes told her the tactic she'd decided to use was having its effect.

The man in charge reached into his interior jacket pocket and pulled out his cell phone. "Parker."

About that same time her overinterested captor had discovered the phone in her back pocket. He leaned close to her and tugged it out, then dropped it into the pocket of his jacket.

You could always tell the difference between undercover operatives and those who were paid to capture and transport targets.

The latter always overdressed for the occasion. Suits and ties and shiny leather shoes. Please, this was awfully dirty work for such businesslike attire.

"He wants to see them first."

This announcement came from the man who'd just tucked his phone back into his pocket.

She and Landry exchanged a knowing look.

Time for that debrief they'd fully expected.

The man moving his hands down her thighs abruptly stopped and stood, the triumphant glitter in his eyes letting her know how much he'd enjoyed his little game. She'd enjoyed it, too. He would soon know just how much.

"Turn around and start walking," the boss ordered. "I think you know where to go. No sudden moves."

She took her time, let the various possibilities for making an unexpected move play out in her head. Since the odds were looking like about five or more to two, they weren't that good. But she'd take her chances.

No way was she going to die without trying.

Chapter 15

With her new friend one step behind her, Olivia moved down the hillside toward the Mercedes and the limo.

Landry's shadow ushered him down the hill, while the one who'd given the orders moved ahead to meet the real men in charge and to receive additional instructions, most likely.

Olivia forced her muscles to relax, allowed herself to bump into her guard once or twice as if she were unsteady. He grabbed her by the arm with his right hand and yanked her closer, purposely jabbing the muzzle of his weapon deeper into her side. She didn't resist. In fact, she kept the arm he'd manacled tucked close to her body, ensuring that his brutal fingers brushed the side of her breast.

She knew he liked it and she would use that to her advantage. A woman could always count on that one basic weakness in a man. Let him believe he was in control and you could lead him anywhere. The feel of the overlooked knife in her shoe provided undeniable evidence of her deduction.

As they neared the lower parking area near the manmade lake, the men who waited next to the limo turned to watch their arrival.

Olivia had known this moment was coming. She'd thought she was prepared for the reality.

But she wasn't.

When Deputy Director David Hamilton's gaze settled upon hers the rush of fury that lashed through her was like nothing she'd ever experienced.

It was him.

She'd refused to believe it…but it was true.

The loss of her life and career three years ago hadn't been about Landry or anything he had or hadn't done. It had been about the bastard standing before her at this moment. Hamilton and his cohort, Echols. The idea that the president had likely been in on it, as well, made her sick to her stomach.

"You set me up."

Outwardly unfazed by her accusation, Hamilton merely shook his head. "I tried to protect you, Vanessa. I gave you a way out and you refused to stay dead."

"You—"

The rest of her words died in her throat when her keeper's fingers dived into her hair and snapped her head back. "That's enough," he growled.

Hamilton shifted his attention to Landry. "As for you, Landry, you and your former superior should have stayed out of our business. I'd intended to take care of the three of you together, but, unfortunately, he wouldn't wait. I'm certain his body will never be found."

Olivia watched Landry from the edge of her vision; turning her head was impossible. He and Andrew Page had been close. Though he kept his emotions masked behind that cool, calm exterior, she knew he was ready to take Hamilton apart.

Talk about a sucky ending.

"I guarantee yours will be found," Landry returned, the threat delivered so softly but with such lethal precision that even Hamilton flinched.

"Enough chitchat." Hamilton turned his attention to the lead gorilla. "Kill them."

"Wait!" Echols barged into Hamilton's personal space. "You're not going to kill them here, are you?"

Hamilton narrowed his gaze at the younger man. "That's what you wanted, isn't it? You ordered me to eliminate anyone who had knowledge of the Al Hadi mission. Isn't that right?"

Olivia tensed. Hamilton's urging her to trust him...no matter what happened, nudged at her instincts.

Echols rubbed the back of his hand over his mouth

as if somehow the move would prompt the proper response. "Well, yes, but not here." He scanned the deserted park, with its encroaching forest and expansive lake. "Anyone could be hiding in those trees. We don't need any witnesses that can connect the two of us to this." He glanced in Olivia's direction but quickly looked away. "Where's your discretion, man? The president can't afford this kind of scandal. The coming alliance is far too important. We can't allow any risks. The elimination of two..." His voice faltered as he glanced at Olivia and Landry. "Some sacrifice is necessary, as you well know."

Hamilton nodded. "Of course. However, I would have felt more confident had I received these orders directly from the president."

Echols's expression grew more flustered. "You know how busy he is, Hamilton. He has no time for these trivial matters. That's why he has you and me. He doesn't need to be involved."

Olivia didn't know about Landry but she was damn tired of being considered a mere sacrifice.

All she needed was one split second. A single opportunity facilitated by distraction.

If fate wasn't going to hand her one, she'd just have to make her own.

Her guard still had his fingers coiled tightly in her hair. Still had her pulled firmly against his body, the muzzle of his weapon jammed into her rib cage.

Might as well make the best of it.

She eased slightly to the left, aligned her butt

better with his aroused lower anatomy. Either the guy got off on causing pain or her plan had worked to this point. Careful not to make any sudden moves, she pressed her bottom more firmly into him. His fingers tightened in her hair but he made no move to push her away. If anything, he grew harder.

"If the president wants these two dead," Hamilton was saying, "let's get it done. I have other business to attend to this morning."

Olivia heard parts of the conversation but mostly she was focused on how she could make this guy's horniness work for her.

If she moved abruptly he'd surely shoot.

The gun was poking her rib cage on the left. Twisting right would work but she might not be able to move quickly enough. Did she have another alternative?

Landry beat her to the punch.

He and the guy holding him at gunpoint were suddenly on the ground.

Olivia's keeper shifted slightly to see what was going on with his pal. The pressure from his weapon eased a fraction.

Olivia twisted to the right. Hurled herself around behind him, ignoring his grip in her hair. She reached between his legs and grabbed his scrotum with her left hand and the knife with her right.

His weapon discharged.

The bullet whizzed right past her forehead, which was sort of wrenched down to his side.

He howled as she squeezed harder.

His weapon discharged again and hit the ground.

Another shot echoed from somewhere but she couldn't see the source.

She shoved her keeper forward, sending him off balance and to the ground. She scrambled for his weapon but didn't make it.

The third man, the one who'd appeared to be in charge, was suddenly on top of her. He held her against the ground with one hand and aimed the weapon at her head with the other.

Fuck him. She wasn't dying without taking him with her. Careful not to take her eyes off his, she moved her right hand into the best position she could for driving the knife into whatever part of him she could reach.

A heavy foot came down on her hand, pinning her weapon to the ground.

"Let her up," Hamilton ordered.

Olivia's gaze jerked up to his.

"Yes, sir," the gorilla relented.

The pressure on her throat ceased. The guy on top of her got up and backed away.

"Leave the knife on the ground, Vanessa, and get on your feet."

Her fingers unclenched, allowing the knife to drop to the ground. He kicked it aside then offered his hand.

She knocked it away and got up under her own steam.

Apparently several things had happened while she was rolling around on the ground.

Landry was on his feet, looking no worse for wear. His former keeper had a busted lip and a swelling eye. The man she'd given a good squeeze was over in the treeline puking his guts out.

It was the newcomer to the party that confused her. At first she didn't recognize him. Then he spoke. She could have identified that British accent anywhere. Andrew Page. He was far more handsome than his picture.

But wasn't he supposed to be dead?

"Excellent job, Hamilton," Page commented with a smile, the weapon he brandished aimed directly at the head of Paul Echols who was, by the way, currently on his knees pleading for his life. What the hell was going on?

Landry looked from Page to Hamilton and back. "Does anyone care to let us in on the joke?"

Landry's own accent reared its charming head when in the company of a fellow Brit, it seemed. Olivia felt a little quiver ripple through her muscles.

Echols's pleas grew louder.

She still didn't get this.

Hamilton frowned. "Would someone please gag that fool until he's taken away?"

The only one of the three guys who hadn't been injured jumped to obey. He yanked off his tie and silenced Echols. Olivia decided that there was something to be said for dressing up for the occasion.

When Echols had been restricted to a muffled moaning, Hamilton went on, "I apologize for the inconvenience this operation has caused the two of you. Andrew assures me that neither of you was in actual danger."

Olivia clamped her fingers into balls at her sides and hoped like hell she'd be able to resist slugging one or both men. Not in danger? She thought about the raid at the hotel and what had just happened… they could have been killed!

"Which is more than I can say," he went on, "for the men I had assigned to track your movements and bring you in." He cut a look at Olivia when he said this.

Okay, so she'd shot a couple of guys. She thought they were trying to kill them. Anyone here would have done the same thing.

"So sue me," she tossed at Hamilton. "You should have let us in on whatever the hell was going on. By the way, what the hell is going on?"

"According to Andrew, this operation had to appear real," Hamilton explained. "I wasn't even informed until twenty-four hours ago. Apparently the powers that be at Interpol as well as my own agency were convinced that if Echols was to be cornered, everyone involved had to believe this was the real thing."

Olivia glared at the blithering idiot on the ground who'd begun to cry since he could no longer plead for mercy.

"Why don't we start at the beginning," Landry suggested as he dusted off his clothes.

"Good idea," Olivia chimed in.

The guy who'd been puking had regained his composure and returned to the group. He shot Olivia a nasty look, to which she responded with a wink. This did not appear to make him happy. He and his cohort, the one with the busted lip and rapidly swelling eye, loaded Echols into the limo and climbed in to keep him company.

Page came over to pat his colleague on the back and offer platitudes while Hamilton appeared to gather his thoughts. Or maybe he was trying to figure out a graceful way to say what had to be said.

"Our friend Echols," Hamilton said, resuming his explanation, "took it upon himself three years ago to clear a way for the former White House administration to do business with Al Hadi. Echols made this his personal mission. He wanted to ensure his advancement. But Al Hadi backed out on the bargain. He refused to submit to the numerous compromises in Echols's proposed deal. Echols was infuriated and embarrassed. He decided the only way to save face was to doctor information he provided to the president, causing the former president to agree to an off-the-record elimination of brewing trouble."

"My final mission." Olivia filled in the blank.

Hamilton nodded. "Yes. Echols knew that all hell would break out in political and media circles, so he hatched a plan beforehand on how to deal with that. He would wait until it was too late to call you back in to tell me that the president had changed his mind. When you, of course, carried out your mission, he threatened to blame the Agency. To blame you."

Landry came over to stand beside her. "So you gave her a way out."

"I couldn't let her take the fall for someone else's mistake."

Hamilton looked tired and old. Olivia realized then what a toll the past three years had taken on him, as well.

"Foolishly I shared my plan with Echols. There was no reason for me to believe that he wasn't on our side. I was under the impression that the president was the one who'd caused this travesty. That mistake came back to haunt me recently when the talk of an alliance, with Echols at the helm, got under way."

Olivia understood. "Echols didn't want to take any chances on one of us coming forward with the truth about what happened."

"Precisely," Page confirmed. "I wanted to tell you the truth," he said to Landry. "But I couldn't risk that the truth would soften your reactions. We needed Echols to believe this was real in order to prompt his confession, otherwise we would have been back at square one. I had to leave you, as well as Hamilton and Woods, guessing."

An epiphany struck. "That clears me." The concept astounded her, shook her.

Hamilton smiled, one of those fatherly gestures.

"That's correct. I'm prepared to fully reinstate you, Vanessa, if you're interested in working for the Agency again. Director Woods will be one hundred percent behind me."

Page raised his eyebrows and sent Hamilton a knowing look. "I would say that full back pay is in order."

"Absolutely," Hamilton agreed.

Olivia couldn't think. She felt overwhelmed.

The adrenaline had deserted her and she suddenly felt every minute of the insanity she'd been through in the past four days.

"Take some time," Hamilton said to her when she failed to give him a ready answer to his offer. "Think about my offer, Vanessa. The Agency could use a woman with your skills."

A number of realizations settled over her just then. Her life was in L.A. now. No question. As nice as it was to know the offer stood, she wasn't interested. "No, thanks, Hamilton. I'm going back to L.A." Saying it out loud felt damn good. "Vanessa Clark is dead. She should stay that way."

He acknowledged her decision with a nod. "Very well, then. I'll see that you get home."

Home. Yep. She was ready to go home.

She told herself not to make the first move, but somehow, after all she'd been through, she couldn't help herself. Her chest felt tight with the need to know what happened next…for them.

Turning her attention to Landry, she asked the

question that burned all the way to the very depths of her soul. "Where do you go from here?"

He took a big breath, let it out. "That depends."

Her heart jolted, sent anticipation soaring through her. Could that mean…? Did she want it to mean his decision depended on *her?* When she would have asked on what, Page stepped in. "I'll need him back in London for a few days." He clapped Landry on the back. "We have things to talk about."

That certainly answered that question. Her heart dropped into her shoes, taking her ability to continue to stand and pretend it didn't matter away in one fell swoop.

Olivia stuck out her hand. "Goodbye, Landry."

He looked startled, which shocked her, but she refused to read anything into it. She was finished trying to read between the lines of the men in her life, past, present or future. She had to get out of here before she embarrassed herself.

He folded his big hand around hers, sending a charge up her arm. "Goodbye, Nessa."

"Olivia," she corrected, determined to make a show of strength.

"Olivia," he acquiesced.

She pulled her hand free of his since he didn't readily let go and turned back to Hamilton. "Get me to L.A., Hamilton. I've had enough of this coast." And there was Jeffrey. She'd have to see that he got home, as well.

They moved toward the Mercedes belonging to

Echols. The limo had already departed with its prisoner and his guards.

Page had ushered Landry to his car. He kept one eye on Olivia until she got into the Mercedes. She knew this because she'd kept an eye on him, as well.

The door closed behind her and the reality that whatever they'd resurrected during this unexpected mission wouldn't matter in the grand scheme of things.

It was over.

All of it.

No point in looking back.

But she did. She couldn't help herself.

She watched the Jag carrying Landry disappear in the other direction as Hamilton pointed the Mercedes toward the city.

No way would she grieve losing Landry again.

She'd done that once.

Besides, she should be happy. The past was really behind her now. She didn't have to fear being recognized. No more evacuation plans were necessary. Her life would finally be normal.

It just wouldn't include the man she loved. But then that had never been the plan…until she'd foolishly let herself hope…again.

Chapter 16

Olivia was dictating notes on her final patient for the day when she heard someone come into the reception area of her West Hollywood office.

She turned off the tape recorder and got up to greet the unexpected visitor. There were no more appointments on her calendar. New patients generally called before showing up at her door.

Jeffrey, sans his usual white lab coat, smiled as she stepped into the room. "I was just leaving your key. I didn't mean to disturb you."

He placed the key to her house on the table between the two chairs that flanked her front window.

"Thanks. I appreciate your dropping it by."

She'd only been back a week. She'd told Jeffrey

not to hurry about moving out but he'd wanted to put this behind him, she supposed. He'd moved the last of his things from her place yesterday.

"You look well."

She was back to being Dr. Olivia Mills. Her hair was arranged in her preferred French twist. The skirt and blouse were classic, as were the stilettos. Her patients paid well for her services. They expected a certain level of elegance in both her office and her attire. New curtains and a fresh paint job were next.

"So do you." That sounded entirely lame, but she had to admit that Jeffrey looked good.

"Excellent." He gestured to the door. "I should go."

Olivia couldn't do this, just stand there and pretend they hadn't shared so much. She walked straight up to him and hugged him fiercely.

He hugged her back.

Eventually she saw him out the door and watched him drive away. They would run into each other from time to time. Despite its size, L.A. and its many communities could be a small world at times. People generally operated in their comfort zones. She'd see Jeffrey at the market or in one of their favored shopping areas. They would both smile and say hello. He would move on, find someone new and maybe get married and have children.

She, on the other hand, could do none of the above.

Her heart was not available.

After turning the sign to Closed and locking the

door, she wandered back to her office and finished dictating her notes.

It wasn't the end of the world.

She had her work.

She had her freedom.

Anything else was icing on the cake.

When she'd finished for the day, she grabbed her handbag and left by the side exit. She drew up short when her gaze landed on Landry leaning against her Audi.

"I would have been here sooner but Andrew insisted on formal ceremonies."

She ordered her heart to stop its fluttering. "Ceremonies?"

He moved one broad shoulder up and down carelessly. "In some circles I'm actually considered a hero. Apparently when I abruptly resigned two years ago, I had several medals coming to me."

She tried so hard not to conduct a visual inventory. She didn't want him to pick up on how thrilled she was to see him.

Her efforts failed. Her gaze took in every detail, from his handsome face to his booted feet. The well-fitting jeans and snug Henley shirt emphasized every sexy feature.

Sweat beaded on her skin.

But the worst betrayal she suffered was the pounding in her chest. She couldn't catch her breath. Couldn't slow down the anticipation building with each passing second.

"Are you enjoying your vacation in our fair city?" She almost cringed at the too high-pitched tone of her voice. No one else had ever been able to do this to her.

"I live here."

Had he told her that? She surely would have remembered. "Really?" She strong-armed her gaze to her Audi and walked over to the driver's-side door and opened it. "I guess I forgot."

"Right here in the Hills. We're practically neighbors."

Well, he had said he'd watched her. Apparently more often than she'd suspected. How was it she'd never run into him?

What was she saying? The guy was a master spy. He wouldn't be seen unless he wanted to be seen. She tossed her bag inside and produced a smile for the man she could feel staring at her. "Welcome back. But, as you can see, I was just on my way home."

He faced her, rested his folded arms on her open door. "Actually, I was planning to take you to dinner."

Hope sang through her veins and she wanted to kick herself. "I'll have to check my schedule." With him this close she couldn't look at him, not without getting lost in those eyes. She knew herself too well.

"I already checked it." He came around the door and trapped her against the car. "You're free. So why don't we stop playing games and say what we really mean?"

"Games?" She manufactured an expression of innocence. "I'm not sure I know what you mean."

"Nes—" He stopped himself, took a breath. "Olivia, you know how I feel. I am brutally aware of how you feel. Let's not do this."

Oh, now *this* she enjoyed. "You sound a little desperate, Landry. We really should take our time plotting our future together. We wouldn't want to rush into anything, would we?"

His hand went to her waist and pulled her against him. He was hard. A thrilling sensation rushed along every nerve ending.

"I've waited three years to get you back. I'm not waiting a minute longer."

She opened her mouth to protest his high-handed tactics but he silenced her with his lips.

Why fight it? She leaned into the kiss, let herself get lost in the taste, smell and feel of him.

Delayed gratification was overrated anyway.

Life was short. She knew firsthand.

Time to start really living.

The drive to his place didn't take that long. He had her half undressed by the time they arrived. They stumbled out of the Audi, and on to his front door, his shirt landing on the sidewalk along the way.

He fumbled with his key...finally managed to get the door open and then she was in his arms again. She wanted to take in his home...to see if it matched the man, but she couldn't think of anything right now but getting naked.

They didn't make it up the stairs…clothes littered the first five or six steps and that was as far as they got.

Landry braced her against the wall, then hoisted her upward as she wrapped her legs around his lean hips.

No words were spoken…the feel of his skin meshed with hers. He completed the connection, stealing her breath and making speech impossible.

This was where she belonged…in his arms…it was the only place she'd ever really belonged.

Finally she was *home*.

And this time, it was going to last.

* * * * *

Silhouette Bombshell keeps getting hotter!
Look out for more fast-paced,
romantic adventures coming your way,
featuring women you'd love to know and the
villains and men who challenge them.

Turn the page for a sneak peek at
one of next month's releases,

WHAT STELLA WANTS
by Nancy Bartholomew

Available July 2006
wherever Silhouette Books are sold.

It was about time my luck changed. In the past month I'd been beaten up, shot at, lied to and seduced. In my opinion, other than the seduction, I'd been on the short end of the karma scale. At least this stakeout and surveillance, while in the middle of winter, was indoors. Okay, so there wasn't any heat in the garage, but I wasn't standing outside in a blizzard, either. And our target was slow-moving and not very dangerous. She was an old lady.

The bad news was, she was my aunt Lucy.

My partner, Jake Carpenter, also known as the man voted most likely to get under my skin and into my bed, was crouched next to me, peering out the grimy garage window and into Aunt Lucy's kitchen.

"She let him in," he said. "Why hasn't she brought him back to the kitchen? She brings everybody to the kitchen."

I looked at Jake. Tall, dark, handsome and sometimes completely clueless. Not much had changed about the man since high school, since he'd left me waiting at the altar in a failed elopement that still echoed like a bad dream in my memory.

"Oh, I don't know, Jake. Do you think they just went straight down the hall to her bedroom, or what?"

I guess the sarcastic tone gave me away. Jake actually managed to look hurt. "You don't have to be so sensitive about it. I was just asking."

I arched an eyebrow and tried not to notice the way his eyes were traveling the length of my body, stopping at all the good parts, the parts that had so readily responded to his touch just hours before.

"Jake, it's my aunt, for God's sake! She's been widowed what, six months, and some mysterious guy from her past surfaces and she doesn't say one word about who it is or what he wants, and you think I shouldn't be so sensitive? He could be a con man. He could be a killer. He could be—"

I stopped, trying to come up with more possibilities, which gave Jake the window he was looking for. "He could be looking to get laid. Aunt Lucy's old, but she isn't dead!"

I punched him, and his responding grunt was loud enough to let me know I hadn't lost my touch. Police training and conditioning is no joke and I wasn't about to let it go by the wayside just because I was no longer a cop. Private investigators need muscles and endurance, too, maybe even more. They don't

have an entire police force ready to back them up—
they just have a partner or two, if they're lucky. Jake
was solid muscle and ex–Special Forces, but he was
only one guy. I was the other half of the team. I
needed to retain my edge…even if we were tailing
only my elderly aunt at this moment.

As we watched, the back door flew open and my
aunt Lucy came rushing down the steps, a white
plastic trash bag in hand and a grim look on her face.
She headed straight for the garage.

"Hide!" I yelped and dived behind a bunch of
boxes.

Jake wasted no time joining me and together we
crouched, waiting for my aunt to pull open the old
wooden door and head for the trash cans that lined
the far wall.

"Nothing good comes of spying on relatives," I
muttered.

"It was your idea," Jake reminded me.

I wanted to smack him but didn't dare with Aunt
Lucy mere seconds from entering the ancient garage.
So I pinched his earlobe, the only readily available,
exposed flesh I could reach.

"Ouch!"

"Shh!"

The garage door creaked open and Aunt Lucy
could be heard walking briskly across the concrete
floor to the battered metal trash cans. She pulled a
lid off, dumped her bag inside it, replaced the lid and
started to stomp off. Without warning, she stopped

parallel to our hiding place, and as we listened, she sniffed, loudly, cautiously, and I was certain she'd discovered us.

"Hmmph!" She snorted. "Nothing worse than the smell of dead fish!"

Then, without further comment, she left, slamming the garage door securely behind her and continuing on her way across the rectangular backyard. A moment late we heard the back-porch door slam and knew we were in the clear.

"Damn, I thought she was going to nail us," Jake said. "The woman's psychic, I swear she is."

My cell phone rang, startling both of us.

"I thought I had it on vibrate." I fished the offender out of my parka pocket and flipped it open. "Valocchi Investigations."

Jake gave me his usual and customary hard look as I said the name. For some reason the man thought that because we were partners, his name should be on the door. I wasn't sure the partnership was permanent, so why change things before I had a feel for the potential duration of it? Look what happened the last time we tried to form a partnership...I'd wound up hurt and alone, trying to explain running away to marry Jake to my disappointed aunt Lucy and uncle Benny. No, I needed to wait this relationship out before I made another foolish commitment.

"Stella, is that you?" The voice, female and anxious, sounded distinctly familiar.

"Yes?"

"Stella, it's Bitsy Blankenship—well, it's Margoulies now, but it was Blankenship. Margrace Llewellen said you'd moved back home and opened a private-investigation office. I need to see you. Right now!"

I closed my eyes. Elizabeth Blankenship. Blond, cheerleader, airhead and high-maintenance in high school. Sounded like nothing had changed, at least not in the maintenance department. I remembered hearing she'd married a junior diplomat and was now leading the high life of embassy parties and overseas assignments. Figured she'd land on her designer heels. But the demanding, "everything's urgent and about me" tone to her voice brought out the rebellious adolescent in me.

"Uh, sorry, Bitsy," I said. "My first available appointment won't be for another…" I opened my eyes and stared up at the old garage rafters, aware of Jack's confused expression because he knew we were next to unemployment in terms of busy. "I guess I could squeeze you in tomorrow, late morning."

"No! I mean, please, Stella, this is an emergency! I need to see you now!"

I signed, pushed the sleeve up on my parka and looked at my watch. It was almost noon. "Okay, I suppose I could see you at two, but I might be a few minutes late. We're in the middle of an important surveillance."

"Two?" Bitsy's anguished wail was almost satisfying, especially when I remembered that Jake had once dated Bitsy, shortly after he'd failed to show for our elopement to Maryland. "Really, Stella, you can't see me any sooner?"

Damn, what did the woman want, blood? "I'm sorry, Bits, two is my absolute earliest time and I'll be pushing it at that."

I could hear the sound of a car's engine in the background as Bitsy considered whether to take the appointment or not. She was driving and I wondered if she was in town yet or on her way from D.C.

"Oh, all right! I'll do two. I suppose I can waste a couple of hours visiting my grandmother in the nursing home or something."

Visiting her grandmother was a waste of time? Oh, I was so glad I was putting Mrs. High-and-Mighty on the back burner!

"Okay. You know where the office is? It's across from the old newsstand, off Main."

"I'll find it. And, Stella, listen, it's really important that you don't tell anybody about this, okay? I don't want anyone to know I'm in town or that we're meeting. It could be a matter of life and death."

I rolled my eyes at Jake. What had he ever seen in this dingbat? Jake frowned and mouthed the words "Who is it?" But I just smiled and shook my head.

"Don't worry. I won't tell a soul. See you at two!"

I snapped the phone shut and smiled even bigger at Jake. "Guess what, partner? Your old girlfriend, Bitsy, is coming to town, and she wants to hire me."

The Marian priestesses were destroyed long ago, but their daughters live on. The time has come for the heiresses to learn of their legacy, to unite the pieces of a powerful mosaic and bring light to a secret their ancestors died to protect.

The Madonna Key

Follow their quests each month.

Lost Calling by Evelyn Vaughn,
July 2006

Haunted Echoes by Cindy Dees,
August 2006

Dark Revelations by Lorna Tedder,
September 2006

Shadow Lines by Carol Stephenson,
October 2006

Hidden Sanctuary by Sharron McClellan,
November 2006

Veiled Legacy by Jenna Mills,
December 2006

Seventh Key by Evelyn Vaughn,
January 2007

**Hidden in the secrets of antiquity,
lies the unimagined truth...**

Introducing

ROGUE Angel™

a brand-new line filled with mystery
and suspense, action and adventure,
and a fascinating look into history.

And it all begins with DESTINY.

In a sealed crypt in
France, where the
terrifying legend of
the beast of Gevaudan
begins to unravel,
Annja Creed discovers
a stunning artifact
that will seal her destiny.

*Available every other
month starting
July 2006, wherever
you buy books.*

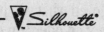

SPECIAL EDITION™

Welcome to Danbury Way—
where nothing is as it seems...

Megan Schumacher has managed to
maintain a low profile on Danbury Way
by keeping the huge success of her
graphics business a secret. But when a
new client turns out to be a neighbor's
sexy ex-husband, rumors of their
developing romance quickly start to swirl.

THE RELUCTANT
CINDERELLA

by CHRISTINE RIMMER

Available July 2006

Don't miss the first book from the
Talk of the Neighborhood miniseries.

Page-turning drama...

Exotic, glamorous locations...

Intense emotion and passionate seduction...

Sheikhs, princes and billionaire tycoons...

This summer, may we suggest:

THE SHEIKH'S DISOBEDIENT BRIDE
by Jane Porter

On sale June.

AT THE GREEK TYCOON'S BIDDING
by Cathy Williams

On sale July.

THE ITALIAN MILLIONAIRE'S VIRGIN WIFE

On sale August.

With new titles to choose from every month,
discover a world of romance in our books written
by internationally bestselling authors.

#97 LOST CALLING—Evelyn Vaughn
The Madonna Key

When a freak Paris earthquake plunged her into a hidden catacomb, museum curator Catrina Dauvergne made an amazing find—remains of the Sisters of Mary, legendary guardians of the Black Madonna. But this career coup made Catrina a target of powerful men set on destroying any trace of these martyrs. Now, as the suspicious earthquakes continued, could Catrina harness the sacred powers of the past to save the future?

#98 PAWN—Carla Cassidy
Athena Force

After testifying against her criminal father, Lynn White had been put to good use as a government agent. Her assignment to stake out Miami's Stingray Wharf was a cakewalk for someone of her special abilities—until she ran into ex-lover Nick Barnes, working undercover to bust a crystal meth ring. The feelings between them were explosive—only overshadowed by the *real* bomb Lynn discovered when her mission turned deadly.

#99 WHAT STELLA WANTS—Nancy Bartholomew

Between her partner Jake's demands for a special place in her business and her heart, and refereeing the romances of her agonizing aunt and New Age cousin, private investigator Stella Valocchi had way too many distractions. But then her high school chum Bitsy bit the dust in an explosion at the mall. Or did she? As Stella worked the case, she realized one thing—life was short, and it was time for her to focus on what *Stella* wanted....

#100 DEAD RECKONING—Sandra K. Moore

To rescue her sister from a drug-smuggling husband, charter-yacht captain Chris Hampton needed backup—bad. When two DEA agents offered to help, it was a godsend, and all three set sail for her brother-in-law's island hideaway. But then the "accidents" began—and when Chris nearly drowned, it was *no* accident. With a double-crossing killer on board, never mind her sister—could Chris save herself from being lost at sea?

SBCNM0606